# SOULLESS

*A Christian Horror*

QUEEN BELINDA VILLARS

ISBN 978-1-954345-07-2 (paperback)
ISBN 978-1-954345-08-9 (digital)



Rushmore Press LLC
1 800 460 9188
www.rushmorepress.com

Printed in the United States of America

# DEDICATED

To my true loves who await me in heaven.
Thank you, God, for creating me.
Thank you, Robert F. Villars, for raising me.
Thank you to the love of my life for loving and guiding me.
You are the keeper of my heart.
I will be reunited with you all when my work here is done.

Annalise listened to the roaring thunder and drops of rain as it hit the rooftop of her small cottage. She remembered that as a child, on days like this, she would meditate on the sound and vibrations of the thunder, always feeling a sense of calmness and peace that she could never feel in silence. Now as a woman twenty-one years of age, she still felt the same way except that the thunder and rain had now given her a sense of strength.

"Annalise!" She heard her mother call out to her in the distance. "My darling, come back to me." Her mother's voice got louder as Annalise shifted focus from the rain to what was going on around her. "You must push or she will die," Sarah, her mother, pleaded.

"I will not! He will take her as soon as she is born," Annalise answered as the thunder continued to roar.

"He will claim her no matter what. If you do not deliver her now, I fear you will both perish," Sarah answered sadly.

Annalise looked down at her large belly. She was in her bedroom on a small uncomfortable bed. Her sheets were soaked with her blood. There were four other women in the room with her—her mother and her triplet aunts Claudia, Claudette, and Claudine. They were all there to assist in the birth of her daughter. She knew she was having a girl before she had even known that she was with a child because her mother had dreamt of the baby constantly. Her mother was known as a seer. Whatever she dreamt came to pass. Annalise grabbed onto her mother's hand tightly when she felt the lower part of her body push on its own.

"No! He'll take her. I won't let him have her!" Annalise shouted.

"My sweet child, you do not have a choice," Sarah whispered softly.

Annalise shut her legs squeezing them tight attempting to keep her baby inside of her where it was safe. She held on as long as she could but knew her baby was coming no matter what. Her aunt Claudine inspected her and saw that her daughter's head was now visible. Annalise closed her eyes and tried to focus on the sound of the thunder and rain again as she felt Claudine pull the baby out of her body, then heard her aunt scurrying to help. She felt as though her heart was being ripped out of her chest when she heard her baby cry. She knew that it would be the first and last time that she would hear such a beautiful sound.

"Give her to me," Annalise demanded.

"Maybe it would be best if we just take her and you don't see what happens next," Sarah said as her sister Claudine handed her the baby.

"Give her to me now, mother!" Annalise insisted.

Her mother carefully put the baby in her arms. Annalise immediately began to sob when she finally held her. She kissed her precious baby, then stared into her eyes for as long as she could, hoping this would leave an imprint on the both of them. That way, they would never forget each other's faces. Her thoughts were interrupted when a strong gust of wind blew her front door open. She looked up and saw a dark hooded figure.

"You know why I am here." The figure said with the voice of a man, but she knew that he was not human.

"You cannot have my child!" Annalise shouted. The door blew shut. The figure slowly moved toward her. He was now standing in the light and surprisingly resembled a human man except his eyes were as black as night.

"Leave here now and no harm will come to you, but you will be leaving alone," Annalise said with authority as she held her baby close to her heart.

"Annalise, you must obey," Sarah begged.

"No, mother! I made no deal with this demon. My daughter will not suffer because of your mistakes," Annalise answered sternly.

"Oh, you are a fiery one." He chuckled. "Ladies, I do not have all night. My master waits for what is rightfully owed to him—

your first-born! Now give her to me." His voice eerily sounded as if multiple people were speaking at once.

"I am not afraid of you, creature. This curse ends now!" Annalise said, then stood up with her baby still in her arms. Although she had just given birth, she now felt an enormous surge of energy move through her body. She was not going to give her daughter up without a fight.

"I am not the one that you should fear. You would be wise not to upset my master. It would mean death to you all, human. This has been the way for centuries. Your firstborn is payment for your very existence. Deny him and you will be destroyed." He smiled.

"Tell your master that he can have her soul when he comes to claim it himself," Annalise answered.

"Enough! I know this is hard. We have all had to endure this. If you do not give her up, we will all be destroyed. Is that what you want?" Her mother implored her but Annalise ignored. She kept her eyes on the creature who never took his gaze off of her daughter.

"Ungrateful slave. You breathe because he allows it. How dare you challenge my master. If he could come here himself, you would be decimated," he hissed. "Her soul belongs to Lucifer and he will have it."

Annalise held on to her baby, then raised her free hand up toward the creature as a surge of energy erupted through the palm of her hand causing the creature to be thrown through the front door of the cottage. His body hit a large oak tree. He was impressed with her strength. He had never witnessed such power in a human before. He arose, then quickly went back into the cottage.

"Nice trick, human, but you are not strong enough to face what is coming if you do not obey," he said, then grabbed her aunt Claudette by her hair forcing her to kneel. "A life for a life. Hand over the child or I will return your aunt to you in pieces." He pulled Claudette's hair causing her to cry out in pain.

"Annalise, please!" Sarah begged.

The creature placed a hand on her aunt's shoulder. Her skin began to melt. She screamed and begged for him to cease. Annalise began to feel faint. She nearly lost her footing but still kept a strong grip on her daughter. The creature sensed that she had no more fight left in her. He knew that her will was strong, but her body was too weak to continue. He released her aunt, then quickly ran over to her. The creature laughed as Annalise tried to push him away. She leaned her weak body against the wall to remain standing. Her body slowly slumped down to the floor. She began to sweat profusely. The creature kneeled down facing her. He gently moved away the pieces of her hair that were in her face and tucked it behind her ear. He sensed her life slipping away.

"I must say, no human has ever put up a fight as you have." He gazed into her green eyes. "How did you acquire such power?"

Annalise could not move. All she could do was hold onto her baby.

"You cannot have them both!" Sarah shouted as she and her sisters joined hands and began to chant a prayer for protection.

"Silence!" The creature shouted, then turned his head glaring at them. The women all fell to the ground and were unable to move. "Time to go child," he said, looking at the baby wrapped in cloth.

"N-no!" Annalise said weakly.

The creature watched as her eyes closed for the last time. Her baby made a sound as if she were laughing, causing him to remove the cloth to see her face. "Ah! There you are. Just as beautiful as your mother. You have her eyes," he said, then moved Annalise's arm so he could take the baby. The newborn smiled at him as he moved to grab her. He suddenly stopped when her eyes turned white.

"Impossible!" he said, then stood up.

The baby let out a piercing scream so powerful it hurt the creature's ears. He scratched at his ears as if he was trying to rip them off. The sound did not affect anyone else but it instantly awakened Annalise. She slowly stood up. Her baby stopped crying. Sarah and her sisters also arose, standing strong. They again began to chant.

"H-h-how does the child possess such power?" the creature asked, still clutching his ears.

"You should be more concerned with what will happen to you next," Annalise said, approaching him. She looked up at her ceiling as a beam of lightning came through, destroying the roof then striking Annalise in her chest. The beam did not hurt her. It moved through her body, then erupted from her hand striking the creature down.

He fell to the ground screaming as it burned through his entire body. Her strength was now replenished. Her mother joined her as she continued to chant. Annalise handed her the baby. Claudia obtained the blood-stained dagger that she used to cut the baby's umbilical cord, then handed it to Annalise.

"Kneel!" Annalise ordered. He immediately obeyed, unable to deny her order. She stood behind him grabbing his head roughly exposing his neck. She then placed the dagger there. Her daughter's blood from the dagger burned through his flesh. "I swear on my soul, your master will *never* have her," she proclaimed as the thunder roared in agreement. She sliced the creature's throat with the dagger, then watched him bleed to death.

"How did you wield such power? You broke our curse. I was wrong. Please forgive me," her mother said, then bowed her head. Her sisters respectfully followed.

"There is nothing to forgive, mother. You did what you and our ancestors were taught to do. For centuries, our people have lived with this curse, but that is over now. Gather our things. We leave at once," Annalise said, then took her baby back into her arms.

"Where are we going?" Sarah asked as the women hurried to get their belongings.

"We're going to see the king and take what is rightfully hers," Annalise answered, cradling her precious daughter. "By the way, mother, that power did not come from me. It came from her, Danara. We shall call her Danara," Annalise proclaimed as she looked deep into her daughter's eyes and saw destiny.

Annalise and her family took all that they could carry to their king's castle. His guards outside of the castle immediately stopped them from entering.

"Get out of here, whore," one of them teased as the other guards laughed. They knew Annalise was one of the king's slaves and he had often had his way with her but when he learned of her pregnancy, he sent her away wanting nothing to do with their unborn child. As they stood there, more guards approached. Annalise knew that there were countless more inside to make sure no one approached the king unless he commanded it. They could all hear the king shouting and laughing from within the castle. He was celebrating his third wedding. He was sixty-six-years-old with no heir, so this time, he married a sixteen-year-old girl hoping she would give him a legitimate son.

"I am not a whore. Our king is the only man I ever laid with and it was *never* with my consent. You all know this to be true," Annalise said, feeling weak again. Just the thought of how the king would force himself inside of her was unbearable. Her daughter playfully pulled her hair, then touched her face. Danara's touch instantly made her mother feel at peace and refocused.

"This is his daughter. She is his only heir. You will let me see him!" Annalise insisted.

One of the guards came forward with his sword raised. "Leave now, slave, while you still have your life or else, I will kill you and your bastard. The new queen will give him a true heir. Now go!" he said, pointing his blade toward her. The other guards drew their swords as well, ready to kill them all. Annalise moved so close to his blade that it nearly touched her. She removed the blanket away from her daughter's face. He looked at the child, then got down on one knee with his head bowed. He held his sword out in both hands before them as if he was making an offering.

"Please forgive me! I pledge my allegiance to your family. From this day forth, my sword is yours," he swore. Annalise allowed him to rise. The other guards were confused. Danara gazed at them causing every knight to pledge their allegiance also.

"Open the gate," he ordered. The massive gates opened.

"More food, more wine!" King Thoron shouted. He was drunk and sweaty. He danced with every woman within his reach, then kissed their breasts. His new bride looked on with disgust.

"You must eat!" The young bride's mother insisted. "King Thoron is repulsive, I know, but he is rich. Your union saved us from poverty. You will show appreciation," her mother whispered, flashing a fake smile at the wedding guest that were watching them closely. "If you displease him in any way, our family will be slaughtered." Her mother urged her to eat again.

"My good people. It is nearly time for me to consummate this marriage." The king cackled with laughter. His young queen cringed and held onto her mother's hand under the table where no one could see.

"My queen, tonight, you will give me an heir!" he shouted, then raised his glass. His wedding guest all raised their glasses cheering.

"You already have an heir, my king." He heard a familiar voice speak. He turned and saw Annalise with his royal guard behind her. The king began to laugh.

"You dare to show your face here slave?" he said walking toward her. "You disrespect my new queen with such lies. *On this day!*" he shouted. "Cease her!" the king ordered.

"Hold-your-position!" The leader of his royal guards ordered the others, disobeying the king. The guards held their position.

"*I gave you an order!*" King Thoron shouted. His guards continued to defy him.

"Has this slave seduced you all?" He laughed.

"Your only heir needs your protection. Claim her, you know I speak the truth. She, Danara, is yours." Annalise said firmly.

"That bastard is not mine! Guards, take them both out of my sight and kill them at once!" he demanded. His guards still would not obey. The king was fueled with anger. His guests were shocked by his guards' resistance. The room fell silent except for the raving king. He grabbed a knife off of his plate of food, but his hand trembled when he heard his daughter cry. He lost his grip and dropped the knife. He felt drawn to his child and reached his arms out. Annalise sensed that he was no longer a threat so she handed Danara to him. The baby stopped crying. As he stared into her white eyes, he not only saw but felt all of the pain he caused her mother. He had forced himself on Annalise for years and tortured her, as he did to many others simply because he could. He never thought of the pain he spread until now. Staring into his daughter's entrancing eyes forced him to see the truth of what a monster he was. Feeling all of his victim's despair brought him to tears.

"Forgive me!" he begged Annalise and handed her their child. He turned away from her ashamed.

"I hereby claim Danara as my one, true heir! Upon my passing, she will inherit my entire kingdom. Serve and protect her as you have done for me. I did not deserve your loyalty, but I thank you all for serving me well," he said loud and clear for all to hear, then faced his young bride.

"Josephine, you are free," he said to the young bride that shortly would no longer be his queen. King Thoron picked up the knife he previously dropped, then again faced Annalise. "It is done," he said, bowing his head.

Annalise remained unmoved as he put the knife on his throat and sliced himself from ear to ear. The wedding guests frantically ran toward the exit doors trampling each other trying to get out. The royal guards rallied around Annalise so no harm would come to her and the baby. Josephine ran over to Annalise. She ordered the guards to let the girl through.

"Thanks to you, I am free!" Josephine said, hugging Annalise tight until her mother rushed her away from the sight of the dying king in a pool of blood.

Annalise kneeled over his body as his blood stained her dress. His breathing ceased once she placed two fingers over his eyes, shutting them forever.

"Danara! Danara!" her mother shouted. Danara giggled as she jumped out from behind a bush and startled her mother. Annalise almost fell as they both laughed.

"This is not the way that a queen conducts herself," Annalise teased.

"May I please play just a little longer? Anius is still hiding in the garden. I must find him or else he will win." Danara pouted.

"I guess a few more minutes wouldn't hurt, but be careful," Annalise said, kissing her daughter's cheek.

Danara immediately ran into the garden maze disappearing from her mother's sight. She was now ten-years-old and was very well-mannered, headstrong, and inquisitive. She liked to think of herself as just a regular girl who happened to be a queen. After the night of her birth, Danara showed no signs of having any abilities. It was as if nothing happened. Annalise was just grateful that her daughter was safe. She and the guards kept a watchful eye on her at all times. They were rich beyond measure, so she spared no expense when it came to her daughter's safety. Although Danara was young, her mother felt it was necessary to tell her the truth of her family's generational curse and how she was the one that broke it. Danara never really believed the stories since she did not feel special nor did she ever witness anything close to what her mother described, but her closest friend Anius believed. Especially since his older sister Josephine was once King Thoron's child bride, Josephine had not been able to return to the castle because the images of the bloody, dying king haunted her. However, she remained eternally grateful to Annalise for freeing her and honoring the agreement that was made between King Thoron and her mother in exchange for Josephine to be his bride. Annalise kindly saved her family from poverty, making Josephine a wealthy widow. Their mother did not feel the same way. She was nervous allowing Anius to be there so frequently but had to comply with what Annalise wanted. Anius and Josephine's mother was still unsure of what happened to King Thoron. He had never presented himself as someone who would take their own life. She and many others thought witchcraft was involved and blamed Annalise. However, they were unable to do anything about it. Since the children were betrothed and would marry when they reached the rightful age, Annalise insisted on them getting to know each other. She was very fond of Anius as was Danara.

"Anius!" Danara searched for him through the massive garden maze.

"Did he come through here?" she whispered to a guard posted nearby. The guard winked at her, then pointed to the direction he saw Anius go. She thanked him, then continued quietly with hopes of sneaking up on her best friend. She passed three more guards, then came upon the center of the maze. This was her favorite place because of the beautiful white lilies that bloomed there. She adored their aroma; it always brought her comfort. She took in a deep breath, then quickly turned around when she heard Anius giggle. She ran back into the maze in his direction, then heard his footsteps just around the corner.

"I win again!" She beamed with excitement as she turned the corner. Anius was not there. She knew he had to be close by.

"Danara!" She heard him whisper from behind the bush. She ran as fast as she could to catch him, but again, he was not there. She saw movement in a nearby bush and quietly crept toward it.

"I got you!" she shouted, then reached both of her arms into the bush and grabbed him.

"You're a cheater. How did you get in there?" She laughed, trying to pull him out.

"Danara! What are you doing?" Anius said, then Danara slowly turned around and saw him standing behind her.

"Anius!—but I thought you were—" she began, but was so shocked she stopped speaking and stared at the bush. Red eyes stared back at her, then arms emerged from the bush and took hold of her pulling her inside. Anius immediately grabbed her legs.

"*Help! Help*!" he shouted, not letting go of her. Danara screamed as three guards appeared, then helped Anius pull her out.

"Your highness, what happened?" the guard asked.

"There was someone in the bush. I . . . I thought it was Anius," Danara answered, then began to cry. "Something grabbed me, it had red eyes—I want my mother." She sobbed. The guards split up. One stayed with the children while the other two inspected the area, plunging their swords into the bushes, finding nothing.

"Something grabbed her. I saw it," Anius backed her story.

"There was no one there. We should get her inside," a guard urged. They quickly walked the children through the maze toward the exit with their swords at hand. Two guards took the lead while one followed behind the children. Danara held on tight to Anius.

"No one will harm you," Anius promised, then put his hand over hers. He could feel her trembling. The guard behind them started screaming. When they looked for him, he was gone. The remaining two guards surrounded the children.

"We must make haste," one guard said and lead the way. They hurried through the maze passing the midpoint. Danara was relieved; she knew now the exit was close. She was startled by another scream, then realized only one guard remained. He grabbed Danara's hand and they began to run.

"*Mother!*" Danara screamed. She had never been so terrified. Annalise and her mother were just outside the maze tending the garden when they heard Danara's distant scream.

"Danara!" Annalise clutched her chest as she and her mother ran toward the maze entrance.

Danara heard her mother yelling and ran faster with Anius and the guard at her side. They suddenly stopped moving when the guard ceased. His sword fell to the ground as the garden came alive. Arms made of thorns reached through the bushes, then pulled the last guard in. His blood splattered all over the children. More thorn arms extended from all angles reaching for them. Anius picked up the fallen guard's sword, then slashed away until they gained an opportunity and fled. They saw the exit as Annalise ran toward them, then her body was suddenly thrown backward, knocking her unconscious. No one was permitted to enter nor leave the maze garden. There was an invisible barrier blocking them. Danara screamed hysterically as the bushes closed in on them and the thorn arms clawed at her. Anius quickly slashed them, freeing her.

"Danara, run, do not look back. I will be right behind you, do not stop!" Anius demanded. She did not hesitate and bolted toward the exit until her feet felt as if they were stuck in the same spot. She looked down at her feet and saw that the ground was caving in. The more she moved, the deeper she sank.

"Danara, do not move!" Annalise shouted when she regained consciousness and saw her precious daughter sinking into the ground. She tried to stand but fell back down. "Please! God in heaven, I beseech you. *Please* hear me, your faithful servant. I beg you, do not let Lucifer take her." She begged on her knees with her hands raised to the sky. She heard Danara yell, then watched powerlessly as her only daughter fell through the ground. Anius without fear jumped into the endless black hole after her.

"Merciful God, let Lucifer take me instead!" Annalise shouted to the sky, surrendering her very soul to God's mercy. Immediately, the sky roared; all clouds cleared out of the way where the sky now turned red. Annalise and her mother stood side by side clutching each other. Neither woman spoke because they were unsure of what they were seeing. A large object shot out of the sky heading toward them, then stopped directly over the garden maze. It resembled an eagle but was all red with golden wings. Its golden beak was so large it could swallow a human whole. God's beautiful beast roared at them, then opened its beak and released a powerful blue flame engulfing the entire maze garden, destroying everything. Again, it roared at Annalise and her mother, then dove down into the ground disappearing into the darkness.

"I failed her. I could not keep her safe." Annalise sobbed in her mother's arms.

"Do not lose hope, Annalise. God has answered your prayer by sending his phoenix. He favors you because you have always been faithful. Remain firm in your belief. He is showing you what your faith and loyalty mean to him. Lucifer cannot have her because God said *no* just as he did the day of her birth. Now pray," her mother said, truly believing. They held hands, bowed their heads, and prayed.

Suddenly, the ground beside them opened up and the phoenix emerged sealing the ground immediately after. The phoenix stood tall before them with its glorious golden wings spread out. Annalise stopped crying when she realized the children were safely tucked under the shadow of each wing. The phoenix gently let the children down. Danara ran into her mother's arms.

"Thank you for saving us." Anius bowed. The phoenix roared, then spoke only to him.

"Take this sword, young warrior. You have earned it." Anius took the large sword made of blue steel. He was surprised at how light the sword was and admired its craftsmanship. He remembered that his late father had a great sword collection that he took great pride in. He had always taken the finest sword from each kingdom he conquered. Each one was special in its own right, but no sword in his father's entire collection could compare to this one.

"This is incredible, phoenix. I cannot accept it. It is meant for a great warrior. I am just a boy," Anius said humbly.

"You are correct, it is meant for a great warrior. God forged this sword with heaven's blue flame and he made it specifically for you. Courage has no age. You have shown more than most men. Your heart is pure and your faith is strong. If God says you are worthy, you are," the phoenix insisted. Anius bowed his head accepting the sword.

"I thank God, truly. I promise to always wield it in his honor," Anius vowed. The phoenix nodded with approval.

"Of that, young warrior, I have no doubt," the phoenix answered.

Annalise approached with her eyes still wet. The phoenix wiped her tears away knowing that she struggled to say the right words to thank God for this blessing. He had worked miracles for her and Danara, yet she still felt unworthy.

"He hears your heart Annalise," the phoenix said sincerely. No more words needed to be spoken.

"Will those creatures ever return? Will I ever see you again?" Danara asked.

"Fear not, child, God will be watching," the phoenix answered, then erupted into the sky disappearing from their sight.

Many years went by. Danara grew up happy and at peace with Anius always at her side. She was now twenty years old and they would soon be married. Anius was twenty-two and had grown into a great leader, but his main priority was his love, Danara. Remaining faithful to his God and keeping her happy and safe were what mattered most to him.

He was running through the halls of her castle when Annalise stopped him.

"Where are you off to in such a hurry?" Annalise asked.

"My brother has just arrived. You know it's been ages since I've seen him," he said excitedly, then kissed her cheek.

"Ugh! You are all sweaty." She wiped her cheek.

"Sorry, I was just training." He laughed, then ran off.

"Well, if you see Danara, please tell her I am looking for her," Annalise concluded.

As soon as he made it outside, Anius already heard his brother's loud voice.

"Big brother!" Anius' brother shouted as he was just dismounting his horse. Anius could tell instantly that years away at war weighed heavily on his brother's face. He had a thick beard and a large scar on his forehead. He had not seen his brother for nearly three years. This made him hug him tighter.

"You are starting to look more like father," Anius joked, tugging his little brother's beard.

"And you're just as tall as I am, but still wet behind the ears," Alexander, his younger brother whom he also called Xander, teased then wiped the sweat off of his brother's head.

"I was just having sword practice. My trainer worked me hard."

"Ah! How is the old fellow?" Xander asked.

"He's retired. I have a new trainer now," Anius answered.

"Well then, let's see what you got. I bet I'm still the better swordsman," he bragged.

"Xander, you were never that good. It's a miracle that you've lasted so long out there," Anius joked as they entered the castle.

"We definitely shall see in a moment. When you are flat on your back, I hope you remember how much you boasted." Xander chuckled. "How is your wife-to-be? I have not seen Danara since she was a little runt chasing you around. I cannot believe we are about to celebrate your wedding."

"I know, right. I've waited a long time for this day to come. She is doing well. She's very excited to see you again," Anius said as they entered the training room.

"Well my, my, my, what do we have here? You did not tell me that your trainer was a woman!" Xander laughed when he saw Anius' trainer in full all-white protective gear from head to toe. Anius and his trainer had been fencing right before his brother arrived.

"Is something funny?" the trainer asked.

"I've just never seen a woman train a man to do anything before, especially not the sword." Xander chuckled. The trainer walked to the middle of the room. Xander immediately admired her curvaceous body.

"Now I see why you have her. Is Danara alright with this?" Xander teased. Anius playfully pushed him.

"So, you think that you can fight better just because you are a man?" she asked.

"Actually, *I know* that I am better. I mean, no offense, but you are just a woman. There is no comparison," Xander answered proudly. Anius looked down and shook his head.

"I see you are still putting your foot in your mouth, little brother," Anius whispered.

"I see you have no manners as well as no sense. Are you going to continue to make me wait?" the trainer asked. Xander laughed at her.

"You certainly have a mouth on you. What exactly am I making you wait for?" Xander asked puzzled.

"I'm waiting for you to come over here and show me how you are better," she replied sternly. Xander burst into laughter.

"Is she serious?" he asked Anius.

"Very! Now would you stop insulting my trainer?" Anius answered.

"Please forgive my ignorant brother, he's been hit on the head quite a few times. I'd also appreciate it if you didn't hurt him," Anius pleaded with her.

"Her? Hurt me? Ha! Now I'm game," Xander said, then joined her.

"Don't worry, since you are the brother of my future king, I will not hurt you too bad," she said, mocking him.

"I'm not worried at all. In fact, I'll even invite you to dinner later if you can knock me down just once," Xander joked.

The trainer quickly dropped down to one knee, then extended her right leg and swiftly pivoted her body around and used her extended right leg to knock Xander's legs away. He hit the floor so hard that he was unaware of what had just happened.

"That was what is called a leg sweep. Now, if you are done babbling, choose your weapon," she said looking down at him. Anius helped his brother get up while trying his best to keep a straight face.

"I cannot believe she knocked me down. Don't tell anyone about this," Xander said shocked. Anius could no longer hold it in, erupting into laughter.

"Are you ready?" she asked with her saber in hand. "Shall I choose your weapon for you?" she said, then walked over to the weapons wall and chose a saber for him as well.

"This is my second favorite weapon because it is light and efficient," she said handing him the saber. "My weapon of choice is the sword, but I don't want to kill you, I just want to put you in your place. So, for now, the saber will have to do," she said, then returned to the middle of the room in fighting stance.

"You better go before she knocks you on your ass again." Anius laughed, then nudged his brother in her direction.

"Alright, you look very serious about this so before this gets out of hand, I do apologize," Xander said in a sarcastic tone. "I still think that men are better fighters and of course, you know I am not going to hit you since you are a woman. So, let's just save you the embarrassment and agree to disagree." He smirked, then noticed Anius put his hand on his face in disbelief. His trainer was now completely offended. She knocked Xander on the back of his head with the edge of her saber. Xander retaliated and swung his saber but she anticipated his move, blocked his hit, then hit him again.

"Your defense is weak," she said swatting his left arm. He struck back. She defended with ease.

"Your left arm is weaker than your right. A true warrior is skilled with both. Allow me to demonstrate," she said, then struck him three more times. Once forcefully on his chest, she then struck both of his arms knocking his saber out of his hand. She caught it midair, then attacked him ferociously with both sabers and once again, knocked him down to the ground. She then sat on his chest with both weapons at his neck.

"Too easy," she boasted.

"Brother, I think I am in love," Xander said smiling. He was in pain yet still mesmerized by her. He watched closely as she removed her protective headgear letting her long dark hair fall down her back.

"Danara!" Annalise shouted from the doorway. "What is the meaning of this?" Annalise continued shouting toward Xander and his brother's trainer.

"He asked for it, mother," Danara answered, then got off of Xander, extended her hand, and helped him up.

"Wait a minute! You're *Danara*?" Xander asked surprised.

"Yes, and you Alexander are still an idiot, just as I remembered," Danara said, then kissed her soon-to-be brother-in-law on the cheek. "Welcome!" she said as he watched her walk away.

"Why must you act so vulgar? You are a queen and should always conduct yourself as such," Annalise scolded as Danara ignored her.

"I am going to have a bath, my love," Danara said, then kissed Anius softly on his lips.

"See you in a bit, beautiful. Do try to stay out of trouble," Anius replied kissing her hand before she walked off.

"Ha! You should tell that to your brother." Danara laughed. Annalise pinched her arm when she walked by.

"Ouch! Mother, you do realize that is an assault to the queen. Guards! Lock her in the dungeon," Danara teased.

"Everything is not a game young lady." Her mother went on as they left the room.

"You know what, it's really annoying how incredibly lucky you are. She is marvelous," Xander said to Anius as they too exited the room.

"Luck has nothing to do with it, Alexander. I am just better than you," Anius teased, then Xander pushed him.

"Seriously, I have missed you. I am very proud of how you've led our army. Father would be proud too," Anius said sincerely.

"Thank you, brother, that means the world to me coming from you. Now, where are the single women and your finest wine?" Xander grinned.

"You have not changed a bit," Anius said, then led the way.

Danara stared at herself in the mirror, amazed. She could not believe that she had just married the man of her dreams and soon, they would solidify their union by making love for the first time.

"You look absolutely beautiful," Annalise said with tears in her eyes.

"Mother, do not cry again," Danara said hugging her.

"I just can't believe you are married. You could not have been blessed with a better husband. Anius is an exceptional man. He will be a wonderful husband and father," Annalise said squeezing her tight.

"Oh mother, he is perfect. I love him so much!" Danara beamed.

"I know you do, darling, I wish your great aunts were still alive. They would be so proud of the queen you have become. Aunt Claudia would say 'be strong for the road ahead'. Aunt Claudette would pray for you to have many sons, and aunt Claudine would be too busy crying to say anything at all," Annalise said, then they both laughed.

"That is so true," Danara agreed, wiping happy tears off of her face. She missed her great aunts dearly. The three of them died mysteriously a few years before, in their sleep on the same night, as if one could not live without the other.

"We had better get you out of your wedding dress, Anius will be here soon," Annalise said right before the guards knocked at her door. Danara's maidens answered the door. It was Anius and Xander.

"I wanted to say goodnight to the beautiful queen and once again welcome you to the family," Xander said, then kissed her hand. Danara gasped at the strong aroma of liquor coming from him.

"Alright, that is enough. Guards, get this drunk to bed in one piece, please," Anius ordered.

"Brother, wait!—I love you," Xander said sloppily kissing his brother's head. Anius chuckled as he walked him toward the hallway. He stopped abruptly as two guards walked past them. Danara also saw the guards walk by and whispered something in her new husband's ear.

"My love, no." Annalise overheard him say.

"What's going on?" she asked.

"Nothing, mother. I would just like to go for a stroll in the garden before we turn in," Danara answered.

"You haven't even changed out of your wedding dress yet," Annalise protested.

"Oh, mother it's fine. I just want to gaze at the stars with my king," Danara lied, then rushed her mother out.

"Guards!" Danara called out to the two guards who had just walked by their room. "Accompany the king and I to the garden," she commanded.

"Yes, your highness," the guards nodded.

Xander watched them walk away. Although he was drunk, he felt in the pit of his stomach that something was wrong.

"I'd like to walk closer to the lake," Danara said as they walked further away from the castle.

"Woman, seriously, we should not do this in your wedding dress, and more importantly, I have waited all of our lives to make sweet love to you but you choose to torture me and make me wait longer." Anius sighed.

"It is just a dress and has served its purpose. I am now your wife so you must listen to everything I say as I will listen to you and do whatever it is you want once we are done with this." Danara smiled, then kissed him passionately and removed his sword from its holster pointing it toward the two guards.

"Were you going to wait until we were asleep and slay us in our bed?" Danara accused the guards. They looked at each other, surprised. One of the guards started shaking, then leaped toward her. Anius quickly grabbed his wife's small dagger that was concealed on her right thigh, then stabbed the guard in the skull, killing him instantly.

"Well now this is not what I had imagined but it is pretty kinky," Xander said as he crept on them with his sword in one hand and a bottle of wine in the other. "I knew you two were up to something but killing your royal guards did not cross my mind. Alright, you two, explain," Xander said, then sat on the ground nearby and sipped his wine.

"Dammit Xander, go back inside. Why did you follow us out here?" Anius asked annoyed.

"Brother, I may be drunk, but my instinct is always sharp. Now, do not deflect. Why on earth are you killing the guards?" Xander said waiting for an answer.

"They were sent here to kill us. They are demons," Danara answered. Xander burst into laughter spilling his wine on himself.

"Demons, you two are just as inebriated as I am." He laughed.

"Xander, we are not drunk. Danara speaks the truth," Anius said keeping a steady eye on the guard.

"You sound as if you actually believe what you are saying." Xander continued to laugh.

"Tonight, the master will have your soul!" the guard shouted at Danara. Xander immediately leaped off of the ground.

"Open your foul mouth again and I will plunge my sword into it," Xander said sternly with his blade so close to the guard's face he dared not move. "Who is this master that you speak of?" he asked.

"He is the father of evil. Your precious queen belongs to him," the guard answered.

"I belong to God," Danara said, then stuck her husband's sword into the guard's heart, slowly. His appearance changed into its true demonic form.

"Tonight, you burn!" the demon said spitting his blood all over her dress. He laughed maniacally until she stuck the sword in deeper, ending its life. Xander fell down on the ground in disbelief.

"D-did you see that? He transformed—I am never drinking again," Xander said taking the last sip of his wine.

"Get up! We need to get back inside," Anius said as he pushed the dead guards' bodies into the lake.

"H-how did you know that thing was not human?" Xander asked still rattled. Danara helped him up and handed Anius his sword. Anius wiped the blood off of her dagger, then carefully lifted her dress returning it to its holster on her thigh.

"I am cursed. Lucifer has hunted me since I was born. His demons dragged me into their pit when I was ten-years-old and Anius jumped in after me. We've been able to see them ever since. The demons are able to inhabit any human's body but they cannot hide from us. There is a darkness that emits from them resembling a shadow that only Anius and I can see," Danara answered.

"This is insane," Xander said shocked.

"Insane, but all true, little brother. Now, let us go. We'll discuss this further inside," Anius said looking around into the darkness. He had an uneasy feeling.

They began to walk, then came to an abrupt halt when they heard screams coming from the castle. Danara knew immediately that her mother was the one screaming. They hastily ran toward the castle. Anius stopped when he realized Danara was no longer running beside him. He saw her surrounded by demons that were coming out of the ground near the lake. One of the demons knocked her unconscious and was dragging her body toward the water. Xander and Anius charged toward them slashing away, killing all in their path. Awaiting hands reached through the water, then pulled Danara in. Once her body was fully submerged, all of the demons disappeared. Anius leaped to dive in after her but the lake completely froze. He punched the frozen water so hard his fists bled. Xander tried to restrain him but his efforts were in vain. Anius continued to pound his bloody fist at the frozen lake until he passed out from exertion.

Danara awoke in total darkness. Her beautiful wedding dress was soaked in blood and water. She sensed movement around her, then was startled by torches suddenly lighting up all around her allowing her to see blood-stained walls made of human body parts. The sight of the human faces was most frightening because of their frozen expressions. Danara thought she heard whispers coming from behind the wall. She got up and moved toward the sound. The air there was so humid. The heat felt overwhelming. She slowly made it over to the wall. Her balance was unsteady. With every second that passed, it became harder for her to breathe. She heard the whispers again and leaned her ear close to the wall. She felt something tug at her hair. Before she could turn around, the wall came alive. Hands clawed at her arms and legs. She felt teeth biting her all over. They chewed on her hair and dress savagely.

"*Enough!*" A male voice shouted. Immediately, everything ceased. The wall was still again. Danara fell to the ground gasping for air.

"Your lungs are collapsing, every breath hurts, but fear not, you will be dead soon," he said calmly, then emerged from the shadows extending his hand to her. She refused his hand.

"Do you know where you are or who I am?" he asked.

"I know you, demon. You are Lucifer," Danara answered, then stood up. She stared at the demon before her with no fear. His appearance was not what she expected. He was human—as beautiful as described in the stories she heard as a child, yet still, evil radiated from him.

"Come with me" he ordered.

She did not move.

"Very well. Stay here and you will be dead within seconds. I assure you it will not be pleasant. You are welcome to stay here, but this time, I will not intervene when those poor souls come out of that wall to rip you to shreds just for a drop of your blood. Trust me, you cannot imagine how thirsty they are," he said in a calm almost soothing tone extending his arm to help her walk.

Again, she refused him. Lucifer walked to a doorway that had just appeared. Danara saw a bright light shining through the door and felt a cool breeze. She slowly followed. Every step became harder. Her chest felt heavy and her ears began to ring. The air was so hot her hair and dress were now dry. Her body gave in and she began to fall. Lucifer caught her before she hit the ground. Her eyes closed for a moment. When she opened them, she was in a massive red cave. The room was surrounded by mirrors at every angle. There was also a large, circular pool next to her that was filled with a strange clear, slimy fluid that swished back and forth on its own. In this room, she was able to breathe with ease. Lucifer sat across from her on a throne also made of human remains. She was startled by his presence since his reflection did not appear in any of the mirrors.

"For years, I have wondered. What is so special about you?" Lucifer began. "When your mother defied me by not turning you over, she broke the curse. You can imagine how frustrated I was. A deal is a deal."

"My mother made no deal with you," Danara answered firmly.

"The deal was made centuries ago by your ancestors. Their firstborn daughters are the payment for your pathetic bloodline to continue to exist. Your spiritually weak ancestors and many others like them believed that God had forsaken them. I tormented them all relentlessly until they pledged the souls of their firstborn daughters to me unknowingly causing a generational curse. Your mother ruined everything; she simply had to comply. Now, look at what has happened," he said, then pointed at the mirrors in front of Danara.

The mirrors lit up all at once showing her entire life from her birth until her last moments on earth.

"I have waited a long time for you. I watched you every day of your life and went through great lengths to get you here," Lucifer spoke as she watched the mirrors. Her heart throbbed when she saw tender moments between her and Anius.

"You-belong-to-me," he whispered in her ear, then swiftly returned to his throne. His movement was so fast her eyes could not follow. His words sent a cold chill down her spine.

"It has been foretold that a girl child will open the doorway for me to return to the miserable world that I have been banished from. Oh, how I long to destroy it! For centuries, I searched for the one that would unleash me onto the world, but Annalise ruined everything by destroying my curse," he went on. As soon as he mentioned her mother's name, the mirrors all began to reflect her mother's life.

"That curse was the only way that I could bring humans down here while they still drew breath. God does not permit such a thing, but those pathetic humans that were weak enough to sacrifice their own to me betrayed him and caused him great pain. In return, he looked away, no longer hearing their prayers. They did this to themselves. I rightfully took what was mine. My minions retrieved the newborn girls, then I extracted their blood and used it to activate this portal. Human blood is more savory and powerful when it's fresh and uncorrupted by me." Lucifer chuckled. "Thus far, I have only been able to send my minions through the portal I created."

Danara no longer paid attention to his rambling. She became fixated on the mirrors that all showed her mother sleeping in her bed as a guard quietly entered her bed-chamber.

"Your presence here changes everything. You most assuredly are the key. When God sent his precious Phoenix down here to retrieve you and Anius, I was truly convinced. There are times that God has intervened for his beloved, ungrateful humans, but never in that nature. For you, he sent one of his most treasured creations," Lucifer said, then once again was upon her. This time, he smelled her hair relishing its sweet scent. Danara's body shuddered.

"This time, my beauty, no one will save you. You are mine for all eternity. I know that you are a stubborn one. You hide your fear of me well, but I know *all*—your every thought, your heart's desire, and your deepest fear. I shall enjoy breaking your strong will," Lucifer said assuredly.

Danara saw that the guard in her mother's room was now standing over her mother's body as she slept. He drew his sword.

"Stop this! You have me here now, leave my mother alone," she pleaded. Lucifer gripped a handful of her hair.

"You are in no position to make demands," he said, then gently ran his middle finger across Danara's throat. Immediately following his actions, the guard ran his sword across her mother's throat. Annalise did not die quickly. She awoke in shock clutching her neck as she slowly choked on her own blood, never knowing her loving daughter had to watch her die unable to save her.

Danara filled with rage swung wildly at Lucifer, then spat in his face as he laughed at her.

"You monster! You killed her! I will never help you. *Never!*" she shouted.

"Help me?" He screamed causing the entire room to shake. He changed form right before her eyes into a hideous monster. He no longer resembled anything close to human.

She wanted to scream but still refused to show fear.

"You are mistaken. I do not need your help. I only require your blood." He hissed and bit into her neck, then carried her weak body to the portal. He forcefully shoved her head into the oily fluid filling it with her blood. He threw her body across the room when he was done with her, then stepped into the portal waiting for it to react but nothing happened.

"No this cannot be, it should have worked." Lucifer stepped out of the portal and pounded his large fist into the fluid. This time, it was she who laughed.

"You will never leave this place. This is where you belong. I will gladly die knowing that you will rot here forever. You are God's only regret." Danara continued to laugh at him.

Lucifer grabbed her, then savagely bit into her neck again smearing her blood on her face. He slammed her body on the ground, lifted her wedding dress, then entered her. Danara screamed and fought him, but he continued. She remembered her dagger concealed on her thigh, then mustered up the energy to reach for it. She plunged her weapon into the side of his neck. He wailed, then his head fell onto her chest. She was relieved to see that he was no longer breathing. She tried to push his body off of hers but he was too heavy. She was horrified when he slowly raised his head hysterically laughing in her face. He then went right back to taking her innocence. She sobbed when she thought of how this was to be her wedding night. She had saved herself for her true love Anius but in an instant, Lucifer destroyed that. She began stabbing him relentlessly until she could no longer move her arms. She cried and prayed for help or death. Her body began to burn inside as Lucifer's blood poured out from the wound that she inflicted on him and fell into her mouth, as he continued to forcefully shove himself inside of her. With each painful thrust, he had taken away everything good that made her who she was. All of the love in her was replaced with hate. Her mind shattered and would forever be consumed with the details of her encounter with evil. His foul scent filled her nostrils. He reeked of death. His bitter blood tasted like despair. His unwanted presence inside of her felt like hopelessness. She was sickened by how much he took pleasure in her misery. She sensed that the more she screamed and cried, the more erect he became. So, she screamed not, she cried not, she felt nothing. Her heart continued to beat but she was emotionally dead inside. Her body no longer felt pain. She felt *nothing* because now she was *nothing*. She closed her eyes hoping it was for the last time.

"Danara!" She heard Anius call her name.

"Anius!" she answered desperately.

"Open your eyes, my love," he said tenderly.

She opened her eyes and saw her husband's beautiful face. He kissed her softly.

"A-Anius how are you here? Where are we?" she asked confused.

"We are home, my love. You fainted when we were out by the lake. You hit your head. How do you feel?" he asked concerned.

"I think—I'm—I had a horrible nightmare but it seemed so real," Danara answered almost in tears.

"You're shaking!"

"I'm alright. I don't want to think about it. Please just hold me. You are all I need." She hugged him.

"You are all I need as well, my beauty," he answered.

Danara looked at him confused. He had never called her that before. That was what Lucifer called her. Anius started chuckling. She looked around, then felt so devastated she screamed but no sound came out. He tricked her. She was still in hell with Lucifer. He was still on top of her defiling her body except now he did so wearing her husband's face. She tried to shut her eyes, but he forced them to stay open as he climaxed.

"This is only the beginning of your eternal hell," he whispered, then kissed her the same way Anius did. He stood up and looked down at her bloody body as she began to gasp for air.

"Do not fight it," Lucifer said now sitting on his throne. "I told you that I would break you. That was nothing compared to the everlasting torment that awaits you, my beauty," he said as she took her last breath and her heart stopped beating. "Finally!" he said excitedly. He waited anxiously for her soul to emerge from her body but nothing happened.

"*Rise!*" he commanded. Her soul remained in her body. Lucifer rose up from his throne of death. There was a loud commotion coming from over his head but he was too concerned with Danara to further investigate. He slowly walked to her body when he heard a low heartbeat.

"Impossible!" he said as he approached. The ground beneath him shook. His minions ran into his chamber.

"Master! What is happening?" his minion asked. Before Lucifer could answer, the walls around them collapsed knocking them all to the ground. He quickly got up looking for Danara's body. He saw a bright blue flame appear through the cloud of smoke and knew immediately that it was Phoenix.

"*She-is-mine!*" Lucifer shouted when he saw Danara in the phoenix's arms and heard the tiny heartbeat pulsing stronger. "This is not your concern. Why do you interfere?" he asked the phoenix angrily.

"*I do not answer to you, demon!* Look at what you have done to God's faithful servant. The time to answer for your sins is near. I hope that I am the one God chooses to *end you!*" the phoenix answered firmly.

"That will never happen. Now put her down and leave. Her soul is rightfully mine!" he shouted.

"If she belongs to you, heaven's traitor, come and claim her," the phoenix dared, then moved toward him.

Lucifer tried to grab her but could not even get close. The phoenix opened his mouth unleashing his powerful blue flame upon Lucifer making him fall to the ground burning. The phoenix stood over him as he burned. The blue flame was the only thing that hurt Lucifer. It was God that made this so. "You are lucky that today is not the day," the phoenix said, then extinguished his flame. "Until next time, demon," the phoenix said turning.

"*No!* Stop! Wait!" Lucifer pleaded, but in an instant, the phoenix and Danara were gone.

Back at the castle, Anius was sick with worry. He had not slept in seven days since Danara's abduction. After the death of Annalise three days before, he buried her, then spent his days intoxicated. He was inconsolable, unable to go on without his love. He longed to take her place in hell or suffer beside her.

"Brother, you should try to eat," Xander pleaded. "I cannot bear to see you like this," Xander said but Anius did not care for his concern.

"You can leave!" Anius said harshly.

"No, how about you eat? Danara would not want you to starve yourself!" Xander yelled.

"*Do not tell me what my wife would have wanted!*" Anius shouted, then threw his wine glass at the fireplace. "I failed her," he said staring at the flame.

"Brother, you did all that you could. We both did, look at me," he begged. Anius looked straight into his brother's eyes.

"Save your words for someone that they can reach. Without my wife, I am lost," Anius said sipping wine from the bottle.

"You are not lost. You still have mother and I and our sister, Josephine. You have a kingdom. Your people are starting to ask questions. They need to know that Danara is not returning. I understand your pain but—" Xander said sincerely. Anius interrupted him and roughly pushed him away.

"You do not understand anything! She was everything! Now she burns with Lucifer. I deserve to burn with her for failing her," he shouted, then again stared at the fireplace. He became entranced by the fire.

"Anius!" He heard a soothing familiar voice speak from the fire.

"Did you hear that? Who is that?" he asked Xander, shocked.

"Hear what?" Xander answered.

"Anius, you know with whom you speak," said the voice from the flame.

"Phoenix?" Anius responded moving closer to the fireplace.

"Brother, who are you talking to?" Xander was perplexed.

"Come forward," the flame spoke. Anius obeyed.

Xander was taken aback when he saw the fire grow, then turned blue. Anius walked into the blue flame, then disappeared.

The flame took Anius back to the lake where Danara was taken. Phoenix stood before him carrying Danara, then gently placed her body on the ground.

"Danara! Danara!" Anius said as he collapsed to his knees kissing her face. She was unconscious. He checked her pulse. She looked like she was in peaceful sleep, but he knew even before he checked her pulse that she was dead.

"Phoenix, what has Lucifer done to her?" Anius wept when he noticed her torn wedding dress completely covered in blood and saw claw marks all over her arms and legs. Her face was covered with a black fluid and chunks of flesh were missing from her neck.

"I am deeply sorry Anius. Lucifer has done the most unimaginable thing that can be done to a person," the phoenix said sadly. Anius let out a heartbreaking scream that was heard throughout the kingdom. Within seconds, Xander and the royal guards were outside running toward them. The phoenix raised his mighty left wing. Anius instantly noticed the loss of sound. He looked back at his brother and saw him and the guards frozen in place. The phoenix had stopped the time. Anius went back to cradling his beloved as his tears fell down onto her face.

"Listen to my words carefully, faithful human. I can restore her. God will only allow me to heal her outer wounds. She will never be the Danara that you once knew. Lucifer's poisonous blood has seeped inside of her. There is nothing that can cure that," the phoenix explained calmly.

"Please, just bring her back to me. I beg you!" he pleaded.

"There is something I must ask of you first," the phoenix said.

"*Anything*," Anius answered quickly. The phoenix took Anius' hand and placed it on Danara's stomach.

"Do you promise to protect her at all costs? Will you guide her and teach her all that you know? Can you truly accept and love her? If you swear this, your wife will be returned to you." Anius looked at the phoenix with the most sorrowful face ever seen. The phoenix had to maintain composure and be strong for Anius, even though this was deeply heartbreaking. The phoenix could feel all of Anius' anguish and knew that much had been asked of this human, but it was God that required this of Anius and he never gave anyone more than they could bear.

"How . . . how could you ask this of me, or her?" Anius sobbed.

"It is the Almighty God that requires this of you. He will be with you every step of the way as he has always been. You are a firm believer, an honest, righteous man. God has great confidence in you. He chose you for this but the choice to take this difficult path is yours," the phoenix concluded. Anius wiped his tears away.

"I swear on my honor that I will do what God requires until the day that I die," Anius said with great conviction.

The phoenix ignited both Danara and Anius with the blue flame, then vanished. Time unfroze. The blue flame extinguished as Xander and the guards joined them. Anius inspected Danara. She had a pulse but was still unconscious.

"Brother, are you alright? What on earth was that?" Xander asked, then realized Danara was with them. "What? How?" he asked.

Anius got up, then gently picked up his bride. The phoenix was true to word and did restore all of her outer wounds. The blood and scars were gone from her body and her dress. She looked as she did the day she disappeared, but Anius remembered that the phoenix said she would never be the same.

"It's the queen!" the guards said, surprised.

"She's freezing. I must get her inside." Those were the king's only words to them. Once they got inside and he settled her in their bed, Xander sent for the royal physician.

"The physician cannot help her. She will wake up in her own time," Anius said confidently, then started another fire in the fireplace.

"Brother, slow down, you are going to have to explain a few things," Xander said blocking his path. "First off, where did she come from and what was that large creature?"

"It doesn't matter where she came from. She is here now and that was the phoenix sent by God to protect her," Anius answered, then moved Xander out of his way.

"You are going to have to do better than that. You disappeared right in front of me, then reappeared with Danara and a giant bird," Xander went on. His voice began to fade when Anius noticed her eyes had opened. He kneeled over her kissing her hands. She could not speak. She just sobbed looking at his face.

"My love, Phoenix has returned you to me. You don't have to say anything, just rest. You are safe now. I promise I will never again leave your side," Anius vowed. He crawled into the bed next to her and held her close while she cried herself to sleep. Xander left without saying a word. He told the physician when he arrived to give them privacy and to stay close. He had a bad feeling that something was not right with Danara. He hoped for his brother's sake that he was wrong.

Danara slept for the next two days. Anius never left her side as promised. He did not eat nor speak to anyone; he only waited anxiously for her to awaken again. On the third day, she awoke late in the night while Anius slept. She stared at him peculiarly at first, not sure if it was really him or if she truly was home. She put her head on his chest and listened to his heartbeat. This was her Anius. She knew the song of his heart. Lucifer had no heart. She now believed she was home. She quietly got out of the bed, then drank a glass of water that was by their bed. She was so thirsty she drank the entire pitcher. It did not quench her thirst. She felt so cold. She put on her robe that was neatly on the edge of their bed. She saw that she had on her silk nightgown and knew Anius was responsible for this. He always took such good care of her. A cold breeze came in from the balcony's double doors. She rushed over to close it, then noticed her large mirror from the corner of her eye. She looked at her reflection. The first thing she noticed was her favorite lily in her hair. It was called the stargazer; she adored its sweet scent. She took it out of her hair and inhaled the aroma. At this moment, everything felt right in the world. This was one of the reasons why she loved Anius so much. He was always so thoughtful and sweet to her, and he was also good to her mother Annalise. Her heart broke when she thought of how Lucifer had her mother murdered while he made her watch. Lucifer had taken everything from her. Her innocence, her mother, and now Anius. She could not imagine having to look at his face for the rest of her life, not after Lucifer pretended to be her husband. She hoped that their love was strong enough to survive all that had happened, but in her heart, she knew everything had already changed.

"My beauty." Danara heard a whisper coming from the mirror. She thought she had imagined it until she saw the lily in her hand turn black.

"My beauty, can you feel my blood flowing through your veins? We are one now," Lucifer said staring back at her in the mirror. Danara was too terrified to scream.

"Do not fear me. Now I understand why God intervened. Do you not know what you carry inside of you?" He smiled. "From the moment you died, I knew. I heard the child's tiny heartbeat when the phoenix took you from me. You carry my son. Together, we will rule all. Destroy all. You will be my queen and rule at my side."

"*Never! Liar! Deceiver!* I do not carry your abomination. God would never allow such a thing," Danara cried.

"Yet he has, my beauty. Yes, I am a liar, a deceiver. I am the father of all evil but on this, I speak the truth. You carry the key that will set me free to unleash hell on earth," he said proudly.

"I would take my own life before I would ever allow that to happen," she vowed. Lucifer laughed.

"My beauty, this is your destiny. You are the mother of evil. There is nothing you can do to change that. Now that my blood has infected you and you carry my child, you cannot die. Soon, you will become powerful. Everyone around you will suffer, then perish. The thirst you now have can only be quenched by one thing—*blood!*" Danara did not want to believe him, but she knew everything he said was the absolute truth.

"Once you give in and you most assuredly will, the blood will make you stronger. You and my child will need the blood of humans to thrive. I will allow you to remain there until our son is born, then you will return to rule at my side," he continued. Danara felt sick. She was consumed with rage. All she could think of was killing herself and the child. Her face felt hot and her fingers began to tingle. His voice angered her. The thought of his child growing inside of her sickened her.

"I swear to you, demon, I will never be yours. This child will never be yours. You will never escape hell," Danara promised.

"It is already done. Your resistance amuses me. I will enjoy watching you change as your humanity dies."

Danara's stomach began to ache as anger took control. A surge of energy erupted from the palm of her hand shattering the mirror. Anius immediately woke up. Danara took a piece of broken glass and placed it on her wrist.

"Danara, wait! Please, do not do this!" Anius begged.

"You don't understand," she sobbed. "I have to."

"I cannot lose you again. You've just come back to me. Please, put the glass down. Let me help you," he pleaded.

"You cannot help me, just let me die. Lucifer will never leave me alone. You don't know what he did to me." Her voice cracked. Anius slowly moved toward her. "If you knew, you wouldn't want me anymore."

"You know in your heart that nothing could ever make me stop loving you. The phoenix told me what that coward did to you and I promise, I love you still," Anius said in a calm loving tone.

"You . . . you know? Then you must let me end this. Lucifer said that I carry his—" She could not utter the words.

"My love, I already know that you carry his child."

"Then, you know what I must do. I cannot allow this child to live. It is evil. Lucifer will use it to destroy everything and everyone!" Danara screamed and cried. Anius moved closer.

"God will not allow that Danara, I promise you. Before you were restored, the phoenix placed my hand on your stomach and what I felt was not evil. I will keep you both safe. I swore an oath to protect your child. I will love it as my own. Your baby cannot be evil if it comes from you," Anius said sincerely.

"You knew this evil was inside of me and you allowed the phoenix to bring me back? You betrayed me. I do not care about your oath. I will kill this monster." She shouted with so much hate her husband felt it.

"Please forgive me. I could not continue to live without you. When the phoenix told me what happened, I knew this would destroy you, and for a moment, I thought it'd be best if you remained dead, but when the phoenix told me that God chose me for this, I could not say no," Anius said hoping she would understand and trust him as she once did.

"Have you lost your mind? Lucifer took my virginity on our wedding night while he wore your face and now you tell me that you swore an oath to protect his evil child. You are all insane! You have all violated me by taking away my choices. I will *never* forgive you." Danara quickly cut her wrist in front of God, Lucifer, and her husband. By the time Anius reached her, blood was spilling all over the floor.

"Guards! Guards!" Anius shouted. The guards immediately entered the room. He ordered them to fetch the doctor, then he wrapped her wrist with his shirt and applied pressure.

"Let me die," she said weakly.

"Never, my love," he said as the guards returned with the doctor.

"Let me have a look," the doctor said, then removed the shirt from her wrist. She was bleeding heavily. He knew that he had to act fast. The doctor reached over to get his medical bag, but when he returned to close her wounds, they were gone. He sat there with his mouth open in disbelief. Danara saw the shocked look on his face. She looked down, then started screaming.

"Hold her down!" the doctor shouted when he saw her reaching for the glass. Anius immediately stopped her. The blood Danara lost from cutting her wrist began to move. It slithered on the floor making its way to her, then absorbed into her skin. She became hysterical. She was so strong that Anius and the guards struggled to hold her down. The doctor injected a large needle into her arm.

"This will calm her," he said as she quickly fell asleep. Anius placed her back in bed.

"My king, what is happening?" the doctor asked, frightened.

"I need you to keep all that you saw in secret. Is that understood?" Anius demanded.

"Yes, my king, of course" the doctor replied, then bowed.

"Now leave. All of you," Anius commanded. The doctor was the first one out of the room. The guards soon followed. When he was alone with Danara, the broken pieces of the mirror lifted off of the ground again pointing toward him. Anius' eyes turned blue filled with the phoenix's flame.

"Now, it is your turn to leave," Anius said firmly to the demon staring back at him through the broken pieces of the mirror, then controlled the pieces with his mind causing them to reassemble back into the large mirror. He then raised his hand manifesting a blue fireball.

"The phoenix gave you heaven's flame?" Lucifer asked, vexed.

"Yes, the flame is now mine and I know exactly what it does to you, so leave my presence before I use it. My wife and the child are of no concern to you," Anius said filled with so much rage, but he knew that now was not the time for revenge.

"How brave you are with that flame. It's a shame you did not have it when I was taking your wife's virginity." Lucifer smirked trying to provoke him.

"You took something that she never would have given you willingly. You repulse her, know that. Understand, coward, that you will never touch her again and this child will never call you father nor free you from your banishment. Where God has placed you, no man can free you. May you rot eternally in the hell that you created for yourself," Anius said, then before Lucifer could spill another vile word, he used restraint and simply touched the mirror with his blue flame causing it to melt, then disappear. He walked over to the bed where his wife was sleeping peacefully, bent his knees, laid his head near hers, then placed his hand on her belly and prayed.

Danara awoke hours later. She had terrible nightmares of what Lucifer had done to her. Even while asleep, he would not let her be at peace. She grew even more upset seeing that Anius was sleeping beside her peacefully. She thought of how betrayed she felt by him and how Lucifer violated her while he wore her husband's face. She arose from the bed, frantic. She wanted to get away from him. Looking at his face filled her with rage. She forgot about all of their tender moments and how he was there for her since she was a little girl. She could no longer remember their love. In her mind, there was no difference between him and Lucifer. She hated them both. She bumped into the nightstand nearby that had a tray of food on it untouched. She picked up the fork that was neatly beside the plate, then climbed on top of Anius and proceeded to stab his face. Anius woke up screaming. He tried to push her off of him but she was too strong. Xander and the guards rushed into the room and pulled her off of him.

"Release me, you don't understand! I don't want to kill him. I just want to take his face off!" Danara shouted.

"Do not hurt her!" Anius commanded as he held on to his wounded face which was bleeding heavily.

"Take her to my room and restrain her," Xander ordered. The guards obeyed.

"I'm fine!" Anius said as Xander tried to aid him. It was not necessary because Anius used his blue flame to completely heal his wounds.

"How did you do that?" he asked astonished.

"The blue fire is called heaven's flame. The phoenix gave it to me so that I can keep Danara safe," Anius answered feeling restored.

"Why would she attack you? You must give me some answers. I do not understand what is happening," Xander pleaded.

"I will tell you in time, but right now, I cannot leave her alone," Anius said rushing out of the room. Xander followed. Before Anius opened the door to Xander's room, he stopped him.

"Please wait, Danara is not herself right now. She just attacked you. Seeing you now seems like a very bad idea. Let me at least try to calm her," Xander begged him.

Anius knew that his presence would only upset her. He understood why she attacked him. He could sense all of her pain as if her emotions were his own. He decided to let Xander talk to her and remained outside of his door. When Xander entered his room, it was completely dark except for the moonlight shining in. Danara sat still on his bed. He kneeled down in front of her.

"Please tell me what is going on. Why would you attack my brother? I know you love him. He only wants what is best for you. Where did you go? What happened to you?" he asked confused.

"You would never understand," she answered coldly.

"You are my family now. I want to help you. Please make me understand," he said with sincerity. Danara gently grasped his face, then placed his forehead on hers.

"I wish that I could explain everything but it's too horrific for me to ever repeat. Lucifer broke me. I no longer want to live." She began to sob.

Xander's forehead felt warm. He closed his eyes and began to see horrible visions of Danara's encounter with Lucifer. The visions were so real he felt as if he was there. He smelled rotting flesh, felt the heat on his skin, and gasped for air as she did. He saw Annalise's demise and how Lucifer made Danara watch her own mother die as he had her murdered. The kingdom thought Annalise took her own life because of Danara's disappearance, but Anius was adamant that she would never do that. Xander now knew that his brother was right all along. He became overwhelmed with emotion when he saw visions of Lucifer taking her innocence. He desperately wanted to save her in that moment but it had already passed. This was just a memory—a glimpse of the horror she had to endure. Nothing could be done to change things, but now he understood her actions toward his brother. Xander held her closely once the visions ended.

"I . . . I saw everything. I can't explain how, but did . . . did that truly happen? Danara, I am so deeply sorry," he said as tears fell down his face.

"Yes, it all happened. I am doomed, cursed. I now carry Lucifer's child and I do not want it to survive, but my choices have been taken away from me. Now you see why I can't bear to look upon your brother's face." She cried.

"Danara, I do not know the right thing to say but I promise you, I will help you in any way that you need. I swear if I could erase your pain, I would," he professed. She knew that he meant his words. She kissed him softly, then fell into a deep sleep. The two brothers watched over her while she slept. Neither could sleep. Xander vowed to stand by them. He admired his brother's conviction and promised God that he would do everything he could to keep Danara safe.

Danara awoke to whispers in the room. She was still in Xander's bed. He and Anius were nearby whispering.

"How do you feel?" Xander asked as she got up.

"I'm starving!" she replied annoyed when she saw Anius' face still intact. "You are just full of surprises, Anius," she said standing in front of him. She moved his face from side to side inspecting it. She saw no trace of her attack on his face.

"I now have the phoenix's flame. I healed myself with it," he said watching her closely. He did not know if she would attack him or try to hurt herself again but he was ready for anything.

"How fortunate you are to be so favored," she said smugly. "Does it hurt?" she asked touching the side of his face that she had cut.

"No, it's completely healed. I feel no pain," Anius answered.

"Lucky you. My outer wounds are also gone but inside, everything still hurts," she said, then walked out. Anius felt horrible. Her words cut his heart deeply. It was killing him to know that she was suffering and he could not help her.

"Danara, wait," Xander said but she still left. She opened the door and walked past the guards; they followed. "Danara, please give me a moment," Xander said as he followed her down the hallway.

"Relax! I'm not going to hurt anyone or myself. I'm too hungry and besides, I know it's pointless," she answered still walking.

"Listen, you were shouting in your sleep. You said some alarming things," Xander said, but Danara ignored him and walked on.

"Please listen! You said that . . . you said . . ." Xander stuttered, he could not complete his sentence.

"You said that Josephine was going to die," Anius blurted out. Danara stopped walking. She did not reply, she just stood there. She couldn't remember what she dreamt about and did not understand why she would say such a thing about Josephine. She loved her as a sister.

"I would never hurt your sister," she answered truthfully and sincerely.

"We know you would not hurt her. You explained her death in detail. You said her convoy would be attacked and she'd be brutally murdered." Danara stood frozen as Xander went on, "We do not think it was a dream. Could it have been a premonition?"

"I don't know. I cannot remember what I dreamt about last night. I've never had a premonition before. My grandmother was a seer, not me," she answered, but Xander was not convinced. It was chilling, the way she detailed the death of his only sister in her sleep. "I wouldn't dwell on it Xander. Like I said before, I am no seer," she said trying to comfort him.

"But you are not the same, Danara. Remember, I saw what happened to you. From the moment you tasted that monster's blood, it changed you. You cut your wrist, then instantly healed. You have unnatural strength and abilities. So, don't pretend that it would be far-fetched to assume that you had a premonition. Is my sister going to die?" Xander shouted.

"How dare you speak of that!" Danara slapped him. The guards approached, but Anius called them off.

"Please, forgive my brother, Danara. He's been unhinged since we received a raven this morning. The message it carried said that Josephine was on her way here to see you. Her convoy will be here by nightfall," Anius apologized.

Danara now felt very uneasy.

"I swear if I knew that to be true, I would tell you. I don't wish for any harm to befall Josephine." Anius heard truth in her voice.

"Thank you, I believe you. Just to be safe, I sent a few soldiers to meet her. Don't worry, I'm sure she will be fine. You should have something to eat. I'll have the servants draw you a milk bath, if that's alright with you," Anius said so tenderly that she did not protest. She left and the guards followed.

"She knows something," Xander said once she was gone. Anius grabbed him by the throat.

"Never bring up what happened to my wife nor speak to her that way again," he shouted in his brother's face.

"I am sorry I overstepped, but it was with good reason. What if something happens to Josephine?" Xander said afraid for her.

"I said *never*, Alexander!" Anius would not release his grip until he agreed. "You were wrong to assume she would let anything happen to Josephine or even you for that matter. I am the one she wants to hurt. She'd never harm one of you to do so no matter how much she's changed," Anius said, confident in his words.

"I hope you are right," Xander said not as confident.

"I am right! You need a drink. Let us give her some distance. For now, the guards will watch her. Josephine will be here in a few hours, then we can all rest easy," Anius assured him.

"Rest easy! Yeah right. Around here, there is no such thing," Xander said as they walked away.

Danara took a warm milk bath, then tried to eat but the food tasted horrible to her. Even the smell of it made her nauseous. She couldn't get her mind off of Josephine so she decided to go to the training room to work out her aggression. When she entered the room, two guards came in behind her.

"Wait outside. I wish to be alone," she ordered.

"King Anius insisted that we keep a close eye on you," one of her guards answered.

"Hmm! So, you are disobeying my order," she said looking around the room at all the weapons.

"Please, your highness, we mean no disrespect. Your safety is our highest priority. The king said if you protest, he will come to watch over you himself," he answered nervously.

"Alright then, traitors. Live targets it is," Danara said, then grabbed a bow and arrow from the weapons wall. "Grab yourselves a target and hold them up just under your chin," she commanded. The guards gazed at each other, confused.

"You heard me correctly. Go to the center of the room and be sure to stand still or you might catch an arrow in your eye," she said, then smiled. The guards chuckled. They were relieved to see that she was joking. She released an arrow from her bow nearly taking a guard's finger off.

"I know, my aim is off. Trust me I am much better with the sword. I have an idea, you two can walk back and forth with the targets on your arm. I've never used live moving targets before and I do love a good challenge." She smiled again. The guards quickly learned that her smile meant that one of them was going to get hurt. They quickly grabbed the practice targets holding them up.

"How about I let off a few shots to get you moving?" she said, then did exactly that. She released four arrows. Two arrows hit each target but missed the bull's-eye. She reloaded the bow. The guards frantically ran back and forth. One of them caught an arrow in his arm.

"Bull's-eye!" she shouted excitedly. "I'm getting better at this. That time, I actually was aiming for your arm." She laughed. "Now, go to my physician and get that cleaned up. Do not touch that arrow or else you'll bleed out and it won't be pretty," she ordered, then he left and one guard remained.

"So, I'm guessing you want some more!" Danara said reloading.

"I am here to watch over you, your majesty," her guard answered bravely.

"I'm sure you have witnessed the madness that has been happening around here. Do you really think that *you* can protect *me*?" she asked irritated.

"I swore an oath to die if necessary, defending you from any and all enemy threats. I am not afraid of what I have seen nor of what is to come, your highness." He bowed.

"You men and your damn oaths. Alright! Show me how you would fare against all who try to harm me," she said, then grabbed her sword from the weapons wall.

"My queen, I strongly advise against this," he said nervously.

"Are you afraid you might hurt me?" She burst into laughter. "On guard!" she shouted, then swung her sword toward him. He quickly removed his sword from its holster and held it up in defense.

"Come on, make this a little more interesting. *Strike back!*" she shouted.

"My beauty!" She heard Lucifer speak, then looked around frantically for him to appear.

"Your highness, what is wrong? Should I fetch the king?" the guard asked concerned. He saw panic in her eyes as she turned pale. Danara did not answer him. A thick gray fog began to fill the room causing the guard to no longer be visible.

"You must feed the child, my beauty. It grows weak." Lucifer spoke but she could not tell where his voice was coming from.

"Show yourself, coward!" she shouted as her belly began to ache. "I am everywhere, my beauty. All around you and deep inside you." He laughed. Danara put her hands over her ears so she could no longer hear him.

"You cannot hide from me. Mother of my seed. As I told you before, we are now, one!" he shouted. Danara then realized that his voice was coming from inside of her head.

"Leave me alone! I can't take this anymore!" She felt herself becoming unhinged.

"*Feed the child!*" he shouted.

"*Stop it!*" she screamed.

"Danara!" She heard him whisper in the darkness followed by footsteps approaching. "Obey me!" he demanded. "You and the child need blood. Deny me and there will be consequences," he threatened her.

Danara's lips became severely chapped. Her throat was so dry that every breath felt like blades scraping the delicate walls of her esophagus. She took in a deep breath and did not exhale when she heard Lucifer's footsteps suddenly stop right in front of her. He peaked his hideous face through the fog. She could not see his body but that did not deter her from stabbing away at the fog until it disintegrated. Once the room cleared, she saw a figure lying in a pool of blood on its side. She turned the body over. She was shocked to see that the body before her was not Lucifer. It was her brave guard. Lucifer manipulated her into stabbing her guard.

"Please forgive me! I . . . I did not know that it was you, I swear!" she pleaded. She applied pressure to his open chest wound. Blood gushed out so fast it covered her hands and wrists. Its sweet scent entranced her. She wanted to lick his blood off of each finger, slowly. Danara fought her strong urges by focusing on the poor guard. He was suffering terribly and did not want to cry out in pain. He wanted to die like a soldier, honorably.

"I must fetch the doctor!" she said knowing he wouldn't be able to save him; nothing could.

"No, please! You know my wound is fatal. I do not wish to die alone in this room," her guard pleaded.

"*Feed!*" Lucifer shouted in her head again.

Her stomach growled loudly. She felt herself losing control as his blood intoxicated her. His warm blood caused a tingling vibration in her fingertips. She could almost taste it and wanted nothing more than to drain him. She snatched her hands out of his wound ashamed of her thoughts, unintentionally causing his blood to squirt in her face. It dripped down slowly from the top of her forehead past her eye, then moved sensually around her lips touching every curve of her mouth. A single tear dropped from her eye. She wanted desperately to open her mouth and taste his blood, but she knew that would be inhumane and once she tasted it, there would be no turning back. The urge to drink him felt stronger than anything she had ever felt in her entire life. This evil that now existed inside of her was incredibly powerful. Now that she smelled blood and felt its power in her hands, she needed it. Not a single other thought mattered more. She abandoned all reason, licked her lips, and slowly savored it. Waves of pleasure moved throughout her body, satisfying every inch of her. The feeling only lasted a few seconds and now she craved more. She tore into her guard's wound biting him savagely, devouring his warm blood. Danara raised her head as she chewed on his flesh when she heard Lucifer begin to speak to her again.

"Yes! That's a good girl. Now kill him and release his soul to me. With your hellish appetite, you will quickly consume all of these pathetic humans and I will become more powerful than *God*," he said proudly.

"*No one* will *ever* be greater than God," Danara answered believing that wholeheartedly. Even with all that had transpired, she still believed that to be the absolute truth about the Almighty God.

"Thanks to you and my seed, *I will be!*" Lucifer yelled, then appeared to her in the mirrors surrounding her.

"You have no idea how long it takes me to mentally and emotionally break down a human. It is a fun but lengthy process manipulating one into no longer believing in God. Human souls fuel me. You, my beauty, will make this process faster. You will kill them all and I will claim their souls once they are dead. Before, I could only have the undesirable souls and the non-believers that were not worthy of entering the gates of heaven. I am forbidden from physically harming his precious humans but once I break them down mentally and they no longer have faith, they-are-mine! I cause the weak in faith to take their own lives. Humans are so weak-willed it is pathetic. You and I will make a great team. This was always your destiny."

"I did not help you with your portal and I will not help you now!" Danara shouted.

"You do not have a choice. Now that you have tasted the blood, you will not be able to control the urges, cravings, and hunger. You along with my son will become indestructible. Now! Finish this pathetic human," he ordered.

Danara leaned over the guard's body. "I am so sorry," she said, now realizing what she had done.

"I am not sorry. I made a vow to . . . to protect you and I have done that and stayed loyal until the end," her guard said coughing up blood. "I now see the evil you faced. I heard everything he said. You deserve my soul, my queen, not him," he said, then turned his gaze toward Lucifer. "I see you, demon! I learned what you did to my queen the moment the poison in her fangs infected my body. This has reaffirmed my belief in God and I am ever so thankful that he has condemned you to hell where you rightfully belong," the guard said, then spat his blood toward the mirrors that bound Lucifer.

Danara thought carefully of her brave guard's words and of her own experience when she was infected with Lucifer's venomous blood.

"What if I could make you a deal, soldier?" she asked. "Life eternal for your soul," Danara proposed to the guard while staring into Lucifer's eyes as he grew angry.

"Stop this now!" Lucifer demanded.

"What? I can live?" her guard asked eagerly.

"Yes, but you must promise your soul to me," she said now looking at the hopeful guard.

"Queen Danara, I swear to you, my soul is yours," he promised.

Danara smiled at Lucifer as he watched, enraged. She picked up her soldier's sword, then climbed on top of him.

"The deal is made," she said, then put her neck right over the guard's mouth and slit her throat with his sword. Her venomous blood poured into his mouth while she never took her eyes off of Lucifer. She had defied him and knew this would make her stronger than he.

"I will never give a single soul to you, demon. For your child, I will build an army of soulless warriors and they will be your demise," she swore as the wound in her neck closed.

The guard's breath became shallow. His life was fading.

"Now what . . . my queen?" he asked faintly. She kissed her guard's bloody forehead.

"Now-you-die," she said, then bit into his chest wound draining him completely leaving behind only her poisonous blood. He died in her arms. She was surprised that her hunger was still not satisfied after draining him.

"Now rise!" she commanded his soul.

"Do not do this, I forbid it. I command you, Danara!" Lucifer shouted as she slowly approached the mirror. He watched her closely as she raised her right arm. The guard's body immediately began to shake.

"This will not work, my beauty. Only I control their unworthy souls," he said as she ignored him.

"*I said rise!*" she commanded. Suddenly, a white shadow in the image of her guard emerged from his body standing over it.

"Come to me!" Lucifer commanded. The guard's soul glided over to them and stood behind Danara.

"Who do you serve?" she asked without turning to face him.

"I serve the Queen of Souls," her guard's soul answered, then disappeared after he merged his body into hers. Danara turned and let Lucifer watch her walk away. He watched every curve of her body as she moved. As angry as he was, he still wanted her. He was aroused, angry, and proud of her all at the same time. Danara surprised him. No other human had been able to do that. He wanted to destroy her and make her his own. He could not decide which he wanted more and this vexed him further.

"You may rise now. The deal has been fulfilled and my blood has made you immortal," Danara told the guard, then helped him up.

"I am Karo, your highness. I will serve you always." He bowed his head. When he looked down, he saw that his chest wound was healed.

"Danara, I sent these guards to protect you, not for you to torture them," Anius said walking into the room with Xander speaking of the guard she sent to their physician earlier. He stopped talking when he saw blood all over the floor, then noticed blood on her hands and mouth. "Explain!" he said, firmly standing in front of her.

"Your highness, the queen saved my life," Karo interjected.

Danara wanted to speak but could not. She could feel Karo's soul moving through her body. When his soul reached her stomach, she felt full. She understood then that blood only sustained her hunger, it was the soul of humans that satisfied the child. Karo's soul made her power grow. Her eyes turned completely white.

"What's happening to her?" Xander asked nervously.

"She is seeing for the first time," Karo answered with excitement.

"Seeing? How the hell would you know that?" Xander asked.

"She gave me her blood and now I can see what she sees, feel what she feels. She is having a premonition right now," Karo answered. Danara's eyes changed back to their original color. She nearly fell but Anius held her up.

"What did you see?" he asked. Tears of blood fell down her face.

"I saw Josephine. She is in danger. It's happening now, I must go help her," Danara said, then quickly opened the balcony doors and leaped before anyone could stop her. Anius and the others ran to the balcony and were astonished to see her land on the ground unscathed. Without a second thought, Anius jumped off the balcony and landed safely on the ground, then took off running after her. He struggled to keep up. She was incredibly fast.

"We'll follow on horses," Xander said, then he and Karo quickly went to the stables, grabbed their horses, and charged in the direction Anius and Danara were headed. Xander quickly caught up to Anius who had to stop to catch his breath.

"She is too fast!" Anius said.

"Ride with us, Karo can track her," Xander replied.

"No! I'm not pushing hard enough. The phoenix gave me power to protect her. I must learn to wield it," Anius said, then began to run again. Xander and Karo rode beside him at first, then they passed him.

"God, please, help me keep them safe. You chose me to have this power. I know that if it is your will, I trust that you will guide me. I am ready to be your instrument, the guardian of her unborn child," Anius prayed believing that God would hear him. He suddenly felt his legs tingling. He began to run faster and easily passed Xander and Karo. He ran so fast he could now see Danara at a far distance ahead while Xander and Karo were so far behind they looked like two small dots. He continued to run with purpose hoping he could reach Josephine in time.

When Danara reached Josephine's convoy, all of her soldiers were dead. Josephine was nowhere to be found. Only eight filthy bandits remained.

"Where is Princess Josephine?" she asked them angrily.

"Oh, we had no idea we caught us a princess." One of them chuckled.

Danara focused. She sensed Josephine close by. She swiftly passed the man in front of her and went behind the overturned carriage. Josephine was at the bottom of the carriage fighting one of the bandits. He was persistently trying to pull her out. He stabbed her in the leg but she still kept on fighting.

"Release her!" Danara commanded.

"I don't answer to you. Wait your turn, bitch. You are next," he answered as the other men surrounded Danara and the carriage.

"I said release her, at once!" Danara insisted. The bandit now annoyed left Josephine alone and focused on Danara.

"One thing I can't stand is a bitch that doesn't know her place. So, being that you're so pretty, I may let all of my friends here take a turn with you, then I'll carve you up real nice and feed you to our horses," he said spitting next to her. Danara paid no attention to this foul-smelling man. She was busy assessing the situation. There were eight men surrounding her but she sensed four more hidden. Two in a nearby tree and two more hiding behind a multitude of rocks. Josephine began to climb out of the carriage but Danara urged her not to.

"Stay inside, it's for your own safety," she said.

"I am not about to leave you out there with those perverse animals. Where are Anius and your royal guard?" Josephine asked.

"I came alone," Danara answered and watched the bandits take pleasure in knowing that the women were on their own.

"That was very unwise," the bandit said touching her hair smelling its sweet scent. She smiled at him.

"Do you know whose convoy you idiots attacked?" she asked angering them.

"Wench! Our leader Dormont allows us to attack whomever we please. This is our land," he said proudly.

"I am your queen, this is my land. That woman is the sister of my husband, King Anius," she stated. The men began to laugh.

"Really! Then we should keep you both for ransom. I bet the king would pay a high price to get you two back, especially you, your highness. I've never been with a queen. I guess today is my lucky day," he said trying to lick her face. She pushed him away. He slapped her so hard her lip bled. She slowly licked the blood off of her mouth.

"Danara . . . Danara, are you alright?" Josephine asked, then again tried to climb out of the carriage. Danara slammed the carriage door hard, trapping Josephine inside. The man that hit Danara looked down at his fingers. Every finger that touched her blood began to bend backward against his will. His hand was no longer his own. It was hers now and she willed it to destroy him.

"He's dead," the men said panicking.

"If I were you, I would not take another step," she warned, but the proud, stubborn men did not take heed to her words. Every man took a step forward, then felt as if their feet were stuck in the ground. The ground began to rise completely covering their legs until it stopped at their waist.

"I'm stuck!"

"Me too!"

The men were all frantic. She stared at them coldly, then reached her hand out toward them. They all shouted as the ground began to eat them alive. Their screams were so loud and horrific Josephine was frightened to her core. She covered her ears and shut her eyes. The men all felt an intense pain in their chest as Danara paced in front of them.

"I want you to know that I can hear your thoughts. I know all of the horrible things you've done to the innocent and it sickens me." She paced. "You took pleasure in raping, torturing, and killing the defenseless." As she continued, their pain intensified. "Today, you pay for your sins." She stopped pacing. "Lucky for you, you don't get to go to hell because your pathetic souls now belong to me," she said, then all of their hearts ripped out of their chest. The men did not die because Danara did not permit it. She chose one of the hearts that she kept suspended in the air and bit into it. She devoured the heart whole, then licked her fingers afterward.

"Now come to me!" she commanded their souls. Their souls ripped through their bodies tearing away at their flesh obeying the Queen of Souls. The souls entered her body making her feel completely satisfied. When Anius finally caught up to her, he looked at the dead bodies mortified.

"What have you done? Where is Josephine?" he asked hoping his sister was not amongst the dead.

"Fear not, your sister is safe and these pigs got exactly what they deserved," Danara answered, then ripped the door off of the carriage. Anius pulled his hysterical sister out.

"Did they hurt you?" Anius asked as he held his sister in his arms and calmed her.

"Just my leg," she answered trembling in his arms. Anius placed his hand over her wound healing it with heaven's flame. She looked on, amazed.

"I know this must all be very overwhelming, but I promise all will be explained when we get you to safety," Danara said sincerely.

"They . . . they told me that you both were changed but I cannot believe what I just witnessed," Josephine said still in shock.

"They?" Danara and Anius asked at the same time.

"Your aunts. They summoned me. Told me to come here. They said you needed me. At first, I thought that I had gone mad. I've been plagued with nightmares for the past two days. The first night, they came to me and told me that Annalise had passed away. I thought it was just a nightmare. Especially since we did not receive any word from you of this. Then last night, they came to me again and showed me horrible visions of what you endured. I still did not believe until I awoke this morning and your aunts were still with me. They persisted until I agreed to come. Now I see that all they said and showed me were true. I am so very sorry, Danara," Josephine held Danara tight hoping she could feel how much she truly loved her.

"You saved my life just as your aunts said you would. Thank you, sister," Josephine said still hugging her. Danara wanted to push her away at first because her new self now rejected love, but there was an undeniable feeling of comfort in Josephine's arms. She could not help but hug her back.

"I will remain with you to face what is ahead together. I love you Danara," Josephine said dearly.

"I love you too, Josephine," Danara answered truly.

Anius was shocked. This was the first time that he had seen kindness in Danara since she returned to him. This gave him hope that the woman he loved and married was still there.

"Thank you for saving my sister," he said wanting to kiss her.

"There is no need to thank me. She is my family too," she answered looking into his eyes without hate.

"What the hell happened here?" Xander asked riding over to them with Karo at his side. He immediately dismounted his horse and hugged his sister. "Thank the Lord you are safe." He kissed her.

"So, now, seriously guys. What happened?" Xander asked as his eyes could not comprehend what he was looking at. "I mean, were these people?" Xander asked inspecting the bandits' remains. He took out a small knife and picked up what looked like a finger. "Did they explode?" he asked confused causing Danara to chuckle, for once.

"Xander, what is wrong with you? Put that down," Josephine said disgusted with her brother. Instinct gripped Danara's attention suddenly. Anius took notice.

"Are you paying attention?" she asked as they both heard a whistling sound.

"Always, my love," Anius said, then caught an arrow in the air before it could strike his wife. He controlled the arrow with his mind sending it back where it came from toward a nearby tree. The arrow hit the tree igniting it with heaven's flame. Two men fell out of the tree with their bodies on fire.

"I swear you two are just greedy. I could've got those two bastards but you bloodthirsty royals just do not know how to share," Xander ranted like a spoiled child.

"I assure you, brother, there are two more hiding." Anius laughed unable to contain himself. Karo picked up a scent, then immediately ran behind two large boulders.

"Oh no, you don't!" Xander said running after him. Karo devoured the first bandit he saw while Xander stabbed the other in the stomach with his sword. He did not finish him off. He dragged his body toward the others.

"Look, I got one," he boasted. "So, here's what's going to happen to you, piece of shit. Every time I feel like you are lying to me, I'm going to cut off a finger," Xander said standing over the bleeding bandit. "Who ordered you to attack my sister?" he asked. The man spat on him.

"I don't have to tell you shit!" he said causing Xander to cut off two of his fingers, remaining true to his word.

"My apologies. I suck at counting. I am much better at carving." Xander laughed, then tossed his fingers aside.

"Xander, enough. This is barbaric," Josephine said feeling queasy.

"What happened to that pile of remains or whatever that shit is over there was barbaric," he answered his sister, then turned his attention back to the bandit. "I'm not sure what happened to your little friends, but I know they deserve every bit of suffering they got. No one attacks our family and lives," Xander said squeezing the hand that was missing fingers. Anius had enough of this and interjected.

"They saw our banner on the convoy and knew it was royalty they were attacking. That is a declaration of war. Dormont has been condoning this behavior and will be dealt with. Now, finish this," he ordered his brother. Xander quickly obeyed his brother and plunged his sword deep into the bandit's stomach, twisting his blade until he no longer drew breath.

"Feel better now?" Anius asked patting his back playfully.

"Actually yes, I do. What's our next move?" he asked eagerly.

"First thing is getting Josephine to safety," Danara answered.

"We should attack Dormont now!" Xander insisted.

"Calm yourself. He will not get away with this. We have to be sure this was a sanctioned attack and find out if anyone else is involved," Anius answered firmly.

"Anius is correct. We will wait. Dormont is not the only hand in this. Of that, I am sure," Danara said with authority.

"Fine, then how are we to proceed?" Xander asked mounting his horse, then helped Josephine up.

"I have a thought," Josephine chimed in.

"We should invite Dormont over along with the leaders of the neighboring kingdoms. I'm sure we will learn more with them in our presence and look into those that do not show. No one would turn down an invitation from the king and queen," Josephine said.

"Alright, good plan, but how do we get them all to show without arousing suspicion?" Xander asked.

"That's simple. We're going to have a party," Danara concluded.

"My queen, I am sorry. I am doing my best but I'm not sure that I can get this done in time. Your measurements have changed drastically almost as if overnight," Danara's dressmaker complained. She had just finished making her dress for tomorrow's party, but now the queen's breast could not fit in it.

"Everyone out!" Danara shouted. "Except for you." She pointed at the dressmaker.

"Is everything alright, your highness?" her guards asked rushing into her room. Danara took off her shoe, then threw it at the door sending her guards and maidens out of the room.

"Now, as for you. Are you not the royal seamstress?" Danara asked. The nervous old woman shook her head in agreement. "I do understand that I only gave you a week's notice of this party. However, this was your one job and if you are not up to the task, then I have absolutely no use for you other than consuming you for food!" Danara said coldly.

"Danara!" Anius scolded her as he entered the room.

"Goodness! You are always lurking. Can I ever get a moment to myself?" Danara threw her arms up in frustration. Anius couldn't help but notice her very large breasts. He picked up her single shoe by the door, then put it back on her foot.

"Please forgive the queen. She has not been herself lately," Anius apologized to the old dressmaker.

"No worries, my king. I completely understand and will be praying for you. Her temper will only get worse the further the pregnancy goes. I will work on the dress. Hopefully, it will be ready for tomorrow," the old woman said, then left.

"*Hopefully?* You *better* get it done!" Danara shouted.

"She's lucky you showed up when you did. I probably would have drained her," she said to Anius irritated.

"Maybe we should not do this. It's already upsetting you. It's not too late to cancel the party," he said calmly as she opened the balcony doors to get some air.

"No, it's fine. It's not the party that is angering me. It is all of this change happening. I am not in control of any of it. Look at me!" she said trying to squish her breast down. Anius softly chuckled standing behind her.

"You look beautiful. What you are doing to find out why Josephine was attacked is incredible. I cannot thank you enough," he said in a tone that soothes her.

"I look different and I hate it, just reminds me of . . . never mind. Please stop thanking me. I adore Josephine. As for the party, it was bound to happen. It is customary when the king and queen are expecting to have a celebration," she said struggling with all of the emotions she was feeling at once.

"I know, but this is already an impossible situation and I would never want you to feel more pain. I really need you to be sure of this. People will be congratulating us and probably want to rub your stomach. My mother alone will annoy you to death," he said wanting desperately to hold her. Danara took a deep breath, closed her eyes, and exhaled.

"You can," she whispered.

"I can what?" he answered confused.

"You can hold me. In fact, I really need you to right now." Her voice broke. She turned around. He took her into his arms and held her.

"I know the party will not be easy. None of this is," she cried. "I need just one day that I can pretend this child is yours and act like things are normal without constantly thinking about the worst thing that has ever happened to me, and how it destroyed us." She trembled in his safe arms.

"Nothing will ever destroy us, my love. I love you now and forever," he said tenderly.

"Please remind me of that even when I am at my worst. The love that we have shared, I feel it still. I just cannot control my rage and this evil inside me wants to consume me. I am grateful for this moment, for I do not know what will happen in the next." She sobbed.

"Do not dwell on tomorrow, my love. I am grateful for right now. Can I kiss you?" he asked sweetly.

"Yes!" she answered immediately. He kissed her tenderly. It was what they both needed. Everything felt right at this present time. They both knew that soon, it would all change.

The next day, the entire kingdom was abuzz with preparations for the party and excited over the news of the queen's pregnancy. They were even more ecstatic to see her walking through the kingdom with her guards in tow and her servants handing out food to her people. Everyone congratulated her as she walked by so she gave them all the same fake smile. At first, this was difficult for her but she remembered that today was about pretending and this would be the one day the demon could not take away from her. Of course, everyone assumed the father of her child was Anius, so every time someone congratulated her, this made her smile. Her servants continued to hand out food as she and her guards went to visit her mother's grave.

"I need a moment," she told her guards. They gave her some space still keeping her within their view. Danara sat down in front of her mother's grave which already had fresh flowers on it.

"I miss you terribly. You should be here with me right now, mother. Lucifer took you away from me, I promise you I will make him pay dearly for everything," she vowed, holding back her tears. "I love you so much," she said, then stood up. She nearly fell over when she felt pain in her stomach. Her guards quickly came to aid her.

"I am alright. I'm just hungry. Please take me back inside," she said faintly. Her guards rushed her inside taking a back route instead of going through town again, then they sent word to Anius of what happened. He rushed to her room. Her guard stood before her blocking his view of her when he arrived.

"Danara, you gave me such a fright. How are you feeling?" Anius said concerned but happy to see she was alright.

"No need to be troubled, all is well," she said, then her guard immediately fell to the ground. She had completely drained him of all of his blood.

"What have you done?" he said frantically checking the now-deceased guard's pulse.

"Trust me, he is definitely dead," she said without remorse.

"Why would you do this? Yesterday, I thought—" he began, she interrupted him.

"It's the child. I cannot help it. The hunger is so strong I can barely control it," she said feeling light-headed. Anius held her up as the dead guard's soul merged with her body. She instantly felt strong and could stand on her own.

"I told you this child is evil. Blood does not satisfy its hunger. It feeds on souls yet you still think it is innocent." She moved away from him.

"I do not know what to say except that the God I serve has made it clear that this child is meant to be born. Yes, it was created from evil but that does not mean it is evil. We must trust in the Lord," Anius said with conviction.

"Fine! You keep trusting in your God. When this abomination consumes every soul until there is nothing left, what will you say then?" she said walking off ensuring she would have the last word. Once she left, the guard's body ignited into flames, then turned into ash as if he never existed.

The day went by quickly. Guests began to arrive and everyone was pleased with the décor. It had been a while since anyone was allowed in the castle. Danara's mother always kept her away from others besides their own townspeople. All of the guests were now seated and ready to eat. The servants began to serve the food although Danara had not yet joined them.

"Where is the queen?" Dormont asked.

"She will be joining us soon," Anius answered but he was unsure. He had not seen her since earlier when she killed the guard.

"As you all now know, she is expecting so naturally, she has been ill. We will continue to celebrate in her honor," Josephine concurred.

"Oh, but of course, I just assumed she would be a part of the festivities since congratulations are in order for the king and queen." Dormont continued to press them. As soon as he concluded, Danara walked in. The room fell silent.

"Sorry for the delay," she said sincerely. Everyone immediately stood, then bowed their heads as she entered. Anius pulled her chair out for her. They were all mesmerized by her. She wore a stunning gold silk gown that accentuated all of her curves and accommodated her newly large bust that nearly every man could not stop staring at. Anius kissed her hand as she took her seat beside him. Everyone sat down as well.

"You are captivating. The seamstress has done splendid work," Anius said smiling.

"Actually, I drained her, then made this myself," she answered smiling back.

"Danara, please tell me you are not serious," Anius said disappointed.

"Relax, she still has a pulse. Lighten up, it's a party." She giggled.

"That is not funny," he answered.

"Yes, it is!" Josephine chimed in laughing.

"Shame on you for encouraging her. You're just as bad as she is," he said as both women chuckled.

"My queen," Dormont interrupted, "It is good to see you are well. We were all saddened to hear of your mother's passing."

"Thank you, Lord Dormont," Danara answered. Her mood quickly shifted. She made it a point to remind him of his title because she knew this angered him. He like most men in her kingdom hated to see women in power.

"There were rumors that you were missing so I'm very happy to see that they were false," Dormont said smugly.

"The queen was mourning the passing of her mother. Annalise will be missed," Anius toasted. Everyone raised a glass in honor of Annalise. Danara took a sip of her wine watching her guests closely.

"We should also toast to this wonderful new addition to your family. May it be a healthy strong boy that will follow in the footsteps of his father," Dormont's brother Morgan toasted. They all raised their glasses as Danara drank her entire cup and asked for more. Anius could sense her frustration.

"You just say the word and I will end this," he assured her.

"No need to worry about me. I am fine but something is definitely not right," she whispered, then touched her temple causing everyone in the room's eyes to close except two, Dormont and his brother Morgan.

"What . . . what is this?" Dormont asked scared. Danara rose, then tapped Anius on his shoulder. Once he opened his eyes, he knew that she had stopped time and understood that the more souls she consumed, the stronger she became. This troubled him. Danara swiftly made it over to Dormont who was terrified by her movements. She was unnaturally fast. Morgan tried to run but Anius grabbed him and sat him back down.

"You've been a very naughty boy," Danara taunted him.

"You are a witch just as he said," Dormont answered shaking.

"Trust me, I am far worse than a witch. Who told you this? Were you responsible for the attack on Josephine?" she asked, but he was too afraid to answer.

"Tell me now!" she shouted, then stared into his eyes. Dormont almost wet himself when he saw the flames of hell in her eyes.

"It was Lucifer . . . he appeared to us through the mirrors. He ordered us to kill Josephine," he blurted out.

"He said he wants all of you dead. All except you, your highness, because you carry his child," Morgan said. Anius was so enraged he grabbed him by his neck.

"Anius, let him go. We will deal with them accordingly," Danara said calmly, then sat back down. Anius followed, then time unfroze. She sipped her wine as if nothing happened. Dormont and his brother thought that they imagined what just happened but when they looked at their queen, they still saw the fire in her eyes.

"The queen is a witch!" Dormont shouted getting out of his seat. The royal guests were outraged by his outburst.

"It is true! You are being deceived. She carries the devil's child," Morgan shouted.

*"Blasphemy!* How dare you speak ill of the queen," the guest shouted at Dormont and Morgan. Anius and the guards were quickly upon them.

"I should cut out your tongue," Anius said choking Dormont. Xander had his sword drawn on Morgan ready for whatever his brother wanted him to do.

"Confess." Morgan heard Danara whisper in his head. He looked around but she was still in her seat. He stared at all of the angry guests feeling the weight of his actions. This party was attended by all of the neighboring royals. Although he and his brother had two of the largest armies in the kingdom, he knew that if these people united and fought for Danara, he and his brother would assuredly lose.

"Confess!" He heard her whisper again. This time, his lips parted without his consent. "Dormont and I sent mercenaries to attack Josephine's convoy," he blurted out.

"Dear God! Josephine, you were attacked?" Her mother asked nearly in tears.

"Take my family out of here," Anius ordered the guards. They escorted Josephine and her mother out. Danara refused to leave.

"You have just sealed your fate with your confession, coward," Aries said rising out of his seat. He was an old brut, a warrior, and closest friend of Danara's father the late King Thoron. He never said much to Danara. She felt he looked down on her because he thought as her father did about her mother—that she was just a whore, and he was vocal about it when the king passed. He thought Danara did not deserve the crown but he still remained loyal to the throne.

"An attack on the royal family is treason. You should both be beheaded and put on display so others know what happens when you forget your place," Aries said slowly pacing toward Morgan.

"Mind your own business, Aries. I will admit in your day you were an extraordinary swordsman but your time has passed, old man. This is not your fight," Dormont said. Anius tightened his grip on his neck.

"My kingdom, my fight. I do not hide behind an army as you and your useless brother do. As far as my age, time has only enhanced my skills. Give me the opportunity and I will show you," Aries said watching both brothers closely, ready to end them.

"Speaking of our army, I suggest you all take a look outside. If we do not signal our armies, soon they will storm this castle and kill everyone here," Dormont continued. Xander went himself to check, then returned with the grim news. Dormont spoke the truth. Both his and Morgan's armies were outside. Hundreds of soldiers were awaiting their orders.

"You mean to kill us all?" Princess Margot asked. She was from the East and expecting her first child. She now feared for her unborn baby.

"We could kill you all but that is not our intent," Dormont said as Anius took his hand off of his throat.

"We can guarantee you all safe passage if you do one thing," Morgan said. No one asked Morgan what it was but they were all thinking about it and knew whatever he was going to ask of them would be impossible.

"You may all leave right now, in fact. All you have to do is look at our precious queen in the eye and tell her the truth," Morgan went on. "Tell her that she is Lucifer's whore and she carries his child. Do that and you are free to return to your kingdoms and families. You have our word," he promised. Anius lost control and leaped toward Morgan knocking him down on the ground, then punched him in the face repeatedly. It took Xander and four guards to restrain him.

Danara remained silent. Inside her heart was breaking. Not only because of what her people were asked to do but also because she knew Lucifer would never let her go. He would do anything and everything to break her mind and gain control of her. She knew that she could just kill Dormont and Morgan and find some way out of this. Instead, she decided to endure it. She would defy Lucifer again and not allow him to break her nor shame her. She knew this would not be easy but the pain was necessary. From this point on, she had to be hard and as heartless as he was. She would never again give him the satisfaction of hurting her.

"Please do not ask this of us," Princess Margot pleaded. "She is our queen. This is not right!" Margot shouted.

"Does she mean more than your own child?" Dormont asked looking down at her pregnant belly. The princess did not answer; she put her head down in shame. She truly loved her queen, but of course, she loved her baby more and would do anything to protect it.

"Say the words, Margot, for the sake of your child. I . . . I would do it for mine," Danara said sympathetically.

"*No!* I am not going to allow them to treat you like this!" Anius shouted as the guards held him back.

"Please go to our quarters until this is done. No one should die because of me. I can take it. You shouldn't have to, too," she said gently touching her husband's cheek to calm him.

"If you have to endure this, then so shall I," Anius said full of anger.

"Anius, please. I would rather you not be here for this," she pleaded.

"This is not fair. My love, you do not deserve this," he answered.

Danara turned to the guards and ordered them to take Anius to their bed-chamber. He did not go easy. It took several guards to subdue him and drag him away.

"May I sit with you?" Xander asked.

"You should go with your brother. Don't worry about me. Lucifer can't hurt me anymore than he already has," she said confidently.

"I know you are strong and can handle this and I understand that you don't want Anius to suffer. Please allow me to be here in my brother's place. I need to be here for you." Xander was so sincere she allowed him to stay. He sat down beside her as the first person who Dormont chose stepped forward. It was Princess Margot. She was so ashamed she got down on her knees and sobbed. She could not look Danara in the eyes.

"I am so sorry . . . I do not understand why they want us to say these atrocious things. You have always been a remarkable queen. You are loved by us all." She cried. This angered Dormont. He grabbed her by the back of her neck forcing her to stand.

"You bastard!" Aries shouted. Dormont ignored him.

"Say the words or your child dies," he said twisting her neck.

"You will die slow for this!" Xander said wanting to get up and kill him but he imagined how hard this must be for Danara. Instead of acting, he maintained his emotions and held her hand the entire time.

"*Say it!*" Dormont shouted. Princess Margot looked into Danara's eyes which stared back coldly.

"You . . . you are . . . you are Lucifer's whore and you . . . you carry his child," she repeated the words that sickened her.

"Take her to the carriage, then signal the army," Dormont told his brother who quickly obliged.

"Whatever Lucifer promised you for doing this, I can assure you will not live long enough to enjoy it," Xander swore. Dormont knew that he truly meant every word but he felt protected by the devil and trusted in him.

One by one, the royal guests looked at their beloved queen in the eyes, repeated the words, then left. Xander watched Danara's expression closely. Her composure astounded him. She did not show an ounce of emotion. Dormont and Morgan's army did as promised and gave all of the guests safe passage. Aries was the last to go. He refused to say the words.

"You will submit Aries or we will kill your wife and beautiful daughters. You have four girls, right? Maybe I should take one as my bride," Dormont teased.

"Not on my life, you little shit. I should kill you where you stand," Aries said angrily. He then got down on one knee and took Danara's hand.

"Queen Danara, the rightful heir of King Thoron. I have never given you the respect that you deserve and for that, I am sorry. I will not say the words they ask of me. As always, my sword is yours," Aries said and kissed her hand. This made her smile.

"You of all people really surprised me today. I appreciate your loyalty. I do not wish for you or your family to die because of me so please—" she began. Aries would not allow her to continue.

"I would rather die a warrior's death than to say those words to you," he said, then stood up. "You have led this kingdom honorably. Even your asshole father would be proud. In my eyes, that crown is not only your birthright. You earned it," Aries said, then pulled his sword out and pointed it at Dormont.

"I do not fear your threats against my family. My wife and daughters are just as fierce as I am, if not more. Trust me, it is you who should fear them." Aries chuckled.

"Aries, please. Say the words," Danara pleaded fearing for his family.

"My queen, that is one order I will not obey," Aries answered as Morgan returned.

"Stubborn to the end, I presume," Morgan said to Aries. Aries stomped over to Morgan, then roughly pressed his forehead against his.

"You presume right. For it is a man that stands before you. I am a true warrior, something you and your soft brother know nothing about," he answered, then snatched Morgan's sword from its holster startling him. "Take it back if you can," Aries snarled. Morgan did not move.

"I thought not, pussy!" Aries laughed. "Hell awaits me. I will soon find out if the devil bleeds. Let's see how many of your so-called soldiers I will take with me," Aries concluded, then walked out of the room with no fear.

Immediately after his departure, a loud sound came from down the corridor. They all looked on as Anius blew the door open, then stood over his guard's bodies. They all passed out from the blast. Anius' hands were still ignited with the blue flame.

"You wanted a war, you got one!" Anius shouted as he approached. "Remove yourself from my sight. I wish to end you on the battlefield," he said to Dormont confidently.

"You can't possibly think that you will win," Dormont laughed.

"I am certain that you will die," Anius said, then charged into the training room to choose his weapons. Dormont and Morgan left.

"This is exactly what they want. You are walking right into Lucifer's trap," Danara said following him.

"I do not fear Lucifer or those armies. You may have lost your faith in God but mine has never been stronger. We will be victorious," Anius said removing a large ax from the weapons wall. "Stay here with my mother and sister. The archers will remain as well as some soldiers in case they attempt to storm the castle."

"Anius, please don't go," she begged.

"I am your husband. I vowed on our wedding day to love and protect you. I failed you once. There is no way I will fail you again," he said choosing a sphere, then holstering both of his weapons.

"Then I am coming with you," she answered.

"When it comes to your safety, do not deter me. Those men dishonored you. Lucifer thinks he can shame you after all he's done. I am nothing if I stand by and allow him to hurt you again. Now, stand aside. Karo will guard you. We will discuss this no further," Anius answered with authority. He was so angry and focused he did not kiss her goodbye. He glanced at his brother upon his exit. Xander chose a massive war hammer. One side was square with four large spikes; the other side of it had one large spike with a hook on the end. He was ready to wreak havoc.

As Anius rode toward the castle entrance, he felt his heartbeat finally slowed down to a normal, steady pace. He knew not to go into battle with a hot temper, especially not with so many lives in his hands. He looked on at his enemies' enormous army. Instead of feeling intimidated, he was confident because he trusted God and believed this was his purpose, so he did not fear the enemy before him. His elite one-hundred and fifty chariot warriors rode past him and Xander with extra-large chariots that were led by three horses with one man controlling them and another man crouched down hidden behind him. Xander noticed that these men were different from the rest. None of them wore armor or shirts. Their bodies were extremely muscular and had peculiar scars on them. Every last man looked like he had been whipped and burned. This troubled him because he knew torture was not his brother's way of doing things. The chariot warriors all strapped on their unusually large swords, then awaited their king's orders.

"Brother, have these men been tortured?" Xander asked concerned.

"Yes!" Anius answered. "These men were tortured by their own hands. They have dedicated their lives completely to fighting for God. They each saw it fit to be whipped as Jesus Christ was, paying homage to their Lord and Savior for his great sacrifice. They have endured the most rigorous training for years in preparation for this moment to strike a blow against evil," Anius said, then rode to the front of the line. There he saw Aries a short distance away fighting Dormont and Morgan. The brothers were surprised at how strong Aries was for an old man. He attacked them vigorously taking Dormont's left ear before the brothers retreated.

"Vaginas!" Aries shouted at them as they ran to the safety of their army. He then rejoined his.

Anius gave his chariot warriors their orders. They prepared to issue their attack when the ground beneath them began to quake.

"What the hell is that?" Xander asked as a shadow cast over them.

"How about your best warrior against ours?" Morgan shouted as his gift from Lucifer approached—a giant that stood over 20 feet tall.

"We are doomed," Aries said shaking his head. He was not afraid of anything but this beast was like nothing he had ever faced before. He could see no weaknesses and no victory for them.

"What? It's just a damn giant. I've faced two in my time away at war," Xander said proudly.

"We really don't have time for your tall tales right now, Alexander. How are we going to take that down? He can kill us all with one swing," Aries said unnerved.

"Then we give him just one target," Anius said.

"Who? You? You are the king. If you fall, all is lost. Stay back and let us handle this," Xander said.

"How did you fare against such a creature?" Anius asked his brother remaining alert as the giant approached.

"We took one down by attacking his weak spot, his eyes," Xander replied.

"Unfortunately, that's not going to work this time because this giant happens to have a giant fucking helmet." Aries laughed at their misfortune.

"You've got to be kidding me! How did they even make a helmet that size?" Xander was perplexed.

"Well, at least, you will all be having a most glorious death." Aries chuckled.

"Ha! Are you assuming you'll survive?" Xander teased.

"Of course not. I can honestly tell you right now that my death will be shameful. I think I might shit myself," Aries said with a serious face causing the men to erupt into laughter. All except Anius. He remained focused.

"Archers!" Anius shouted. The men fell silent. "When his helmet falls, ignite his eyes with your arrows. As for the rest of you, stand down until further instruction," he commanded, then rode off alone.

Dormont and his brother watched Anius and his men from a safe distance.

"What could they possibly be laughing at?" Dormont asked.

"Who cares, they'll all be dead soon," Morgan answered.

"Is that Anius? He appears to be heading toward the giant, alone." Dormont watched his every move not understanding what the king was up to.

"Maybe Anius has finally gone mad." Morgan was also shocked by his bold move.

"King Anius is too stubborn to lose control. That man is the most strategic warrior we have ever faced. He absolutely has a plan." Dormont watched cautiously.

"I do not understand why you are afraid of Anius. We have Lucifer on our side. He has given us weapons that are unstoppable. There is no way they can even get by our giant, yet still, you worry. He is just a man!" Morgan said irritated.

"It is not the man I fear, but the God he serves."

Anius stood a few feet away from the giant. His war horse Splendor was uneasy but she stood her ground. He stroked her long silky mane gently since this always calmed her.

"Be easy, Splendor. I know he's big but you are a fast girl," he said soothingly.

"She is fast, but she won't be enough to take him down," Xander said joining them. Splendor neighed irritated by his comment.

"You hurt her feelings," Anius joked.

"I could care less about your precious pony's feelings. This is not smart," Xander protested. Splendor stood on her hind legs, then slammed her front hooves down on the ground startling Xander's horse.

"Well, now you've pissed her off. I am very sorry that my brother is an insensitive jerk. Our mother did not hug him enough as a boy," Anius teased patting her gently.

"I'm glad you can joke right now. I really don't understand what you are doing," Xander answered.

"I am leading! Now for once, shut up and follow or stand aside," Anius said, then rode off toward the giant. Xander followed.

"I knew you couldn't stay away," Anius said proudly.

"Someone has to keep your insane ass alive. What's the plan?" Xander asked as they got closer.

"I'm the bait and you are the muscle," Anius answered.

"Oh great. Stupid fucking plan," Xander said sarcastically.

"Trust. This will work. Aim true, brother," Anius said.

"Ride hard, brother," Xander answered, then they both rode around the giant in a circle.

Xander searched frantically for weakness while Anius rode through the giant's legs, then around him in a circular motion agitating the beast. The giant pounded his large fist into the ground missing Anius. The horses were startled but Splendor continued to ride while Xander's horse nearly knocked him off. Anius rode out in front of the giant taunting him. The giant gave chase. Xander followed making his horse get him close, then he leaped onto the giant's right leg and held on tight. Anius stopped Splendor when he saw his brother secure. The giant approached removing his sword which was the length of ten men, then slammed it onto the ground toward Anius. Splendor narrowly evaded. Xander was impressed. He stabbed the giant's ankle but it remained unbothered.

"Did you find a weak spot yet?" Anius asked as he continued to ride circles around the giant.

"Not quite," Xander said as he continued to stab it.

"We just need him to stumble. My archers will do their work. No toes, no balance, brother." Anius laughed.

"I love the way your sick mind works," Xander beamed with excitement. He lowered himself to the giant's feet, then slid into the giant's bootstrap. This kept him from falling off while he began to hack away at its toes. The beast felt this and became irritated. Anius maneuvered Splendor to ride toward Dormont and Morgan's army. He made himself a target for their archers now being in their range of sight.

"Take the shot!" Morgan ordered his archers.

"Wait. What if we hit the giant?" Dormont protested against his plan.

"He can take it. Let's end this now by killing Anius," Morgan said, then ordered his archers to shoot the king down.

Anius and Splendor rode so fast every arrow missed its mark. He rode right by the enemy but the giant now furiously bulldozed through Dormont and Morgan's men crushing many of them causing confusion and chaos. Again, it swung its huge sword toward Anius and missed, but the impact of it hitting the ground knocked every man around it off of their horses, including Anius.

"I'm so sorry girl," Anius said trying to help Splendor up as the giant quickly approached. "I just need you to get me close," he said as she got up and saw that she was hurt.

He mounted her, then she rode with haste toward the giant. The beast swung and missed. Anius seized the chance and stood up on Splendor, then leaped onto the giant's leg joining Xander who was still hacking the beast's toes with his war hammer. The brothers worked together quickly stabbing the giant's toes. The beast roared when they finally began to make progress, then raised his leg and slammed it down knocking Anius off. Xander called out to him but Anius could barely hear. His ears were ringing. He felt his ribs crack when he hit the ground. He tried to stand when he saw the enemy approaching but he fell back down. The giant came toward him from the left while Dormont and his army came from the right side. He looked up to the sky and remembered what he was fighting for and that he was not alone. He watched Dormont and his riders approach, then saw Splendor push through all the other riders reaching him before them all. Anius mounted her, then charged toward the giant.

"Steady," he said calmly as she got closer. "That's it, girl," he said, then grabbed two knives from his boot and provoked the giant to swing again. The giant missed.

"Alright, Splendor, just get me there but not too close," he ordered for her own safety. Splendor disobeyed. She rode onto the giant's sword and up its arm allowing Anius to leap onto the beast safely. The giant knocked Splendor off. Anius used this moment to dig his knives into the giant's flesh climbing it until he reached its neck.

"I think I got one!" Xander shouted from below as he finally severed a toe. The beast roared. Anius took his sword and thrust it into the giant's neck while Xander hacked off another toe. The giant fell to one knee. His helmet hit the ground hard. Anius and Xander dismounted safely. Anius' archers readied their bows, then waited as the beast slowly raised its head with his face now exposed. His archers' aim was true. They flooded the giant's eyes with their arrows until the beast was no more.

"*Kill them both!*" Morgan ordered his riders and they rode toward Anius and his brother who remained there, unmoved. Dormont, bothered by their confidence, looked back and saw why Anius and Xander were not worried. Anius' chariot warriors had given chase and were right behind Dormont, Morgan, and their cavalry. Morgan also saw that they were being chased.

"Don't worry, they're too far. We will kill the king before they reach us," Morgan said confidently. Dormont slowed down his horse, then abandoned his brother and rode away from them when he saw archers rise from behind the chariot warriors with their arrows ignited. They aimed for the sky and shot their fiery arrows. The arrows fell just a few feet away from Anius and Xander. Xander was truly impressed with his brother's tactics and his men when he saw Morgan and his cavalry ride directly through the fire burning nearly all of them while leaving Xander and his brother untouched. Anius' men retrieved him and Xander, then rode back toward the castle.

"You two psychotic bastards actually took the giant down," Aries shouted upon their return as the men cheered. Anius was wounded but he remained focused. He checked on Splendor; she was safe and resting.

"Now, we take out their archers. Sound the horns," Anius ordered. Two of his soldiers came forward with large white horns that resembled elephant tusks. The horns made two different sounds.

One made a high-pitched whistling sound; the other made a thick heavy sound similar to a trumpet. They did this three times.

"What was that for?" Xander asked sipping some water.

"Lysander," Anius answered.

"I had no idea he was still around. How is the old bird?"

"You will see shortly," Anius answered as his medic wrapped his wounds.

Dormont and Morgan gathered their men on the other side of the field opposite Anius' army. They lost half of their army and what pissed off Dormont more was that it was Anius' strategic maneuvering that did it.

"I told you not to underestimate him. Look at how cleverly he used our giant against us," Dormont raved.

"He will still fall!" Morgan answered not as confidently as before. He was badly burned. The two brothers were startled by the sound of horns.

"I don't even want to know what he is up to now. Let us end this," Dormont said mounting his horse.

The sky suddenly made a screeching sound. The winds began to change. A swarm of eagles approached, then stopped just above them.

"What are they doing all together like that? Eagles do not do that," Morgan said shaking.

"Damn the eagles. Anius' chariots are on their way," Dormont answered frantically. Morgan gave their men orders and was ready to ride off when suddenly the swarm of eagles began to attack them. The eagles tore out the men's eyes with their claws and large beaks. Their enormous wings hit multiple men within their range bashing the men continuously without mercy. The eagles decimated their archers, then disappeared into the clouds as Anius' chariot warriors approached. Their horses became agitated by the sudden vibrations emitting from the ground beneath them. They refused to move.

"Fall back!" their king Anius ordered.

His chariot warriors heard him but saw what their king could not. The enemy had giant war machines harnessing large boulders. One boulder had the power to crush the weight of over ten men. They were lined up just over the nearby ridge. There was no time to alert their king. They could have charged toward the machines and easily taken out a huge amount of their enemy soldiers, but that would leave their king open to take the brunt of the enormous boulders that were currently aimed at them. If they charged in at that moment, the enemy would surely then set their aim on Anius. Instead of putting their king in harm's way, they decided as a unit to hold their position. This was an easy unanimous decision. They had all admired their beloved king and queen and this was what they trained for. More importantly on this day, they fought in honor of God. They showed evil that Jesus did not die in vain. They were honored by God's sacrifice and knew at this moment to prove their absolute loyalty to him that they had to die for the man they believed God had chosen, Anius their king. The loud crackle of the boulders being released from Lucifer's death machines echoed throughout the battlefield. The chariot warriors moved as one just as they always did in battle. All dismounted their horses, then looked toward their king. He was at a far distance and sensed immediately that something was wrong.

"I order you to fall back!" Anius shouted. His chariot warriors released their horses sending them toward their king and the rest of his soldiers to keep them all back out of harm's way. When Anius saw this, he ran in their direction knowing full well they were to meet their end. It took ten men to restrain the honorable king that loved each of his men as brothers and would do the same for them. He saw them remove their swords, plant them into the ground, then bend their knees as Xander and his soldiers finally wrestled Anius to the ground. That's when Anius saw the boulders, six of them heading toward his brave, elite men. He understood then what they had done for him. He stopped fighting as their horses rode by him.

"Release me!" he commanded in an undeniable tone.

Xander and his men released him. Anius stood up, raised his right fist, placed it on the left side of his chest, then thrust it into the air pointing toward the heavens saluting them for the last time. His chariot warriors saluted him as well. To them, this salute meant they were taking a piece of his heart with them to heaven. These were men he fought with on the battlefield and shed their blood together. That sacred bond was something only a soldier could understand. His love for his men was absolute. Anius did not look away as the boulders crashed down; he owed them that. The sky began to rumble. Clouds started to ascend from the sky in the shape of two enormous hands. These were the hands of God. He reached out from the heavens and allowed only Anius and his men to witness this miracle. The men looked on astonished as God's hands scorched the earth and obliterated the boulders upon impact. He did not allow one drop of these faithful warriors' blood to spill. They had all honored God. In return, instead of a glorious death, he gave these brave men a glorious welcome into heaven and robbed Lucifer of his victory. In an instant, the chariot warriors were gone. Their enemies were confused. All they saw were the boulders coming down but there were no bodies beneath them.

"Target the king. Do not stop until he is dead," an enraged Morgan ordered all of their men. He and Dormont stayed behind as their soldiers issued the attack. They met Anius and his men on the battlefield and quickly perished.

"Launch the boulders," Morgan ordered.

"We'll hit our own men!" Dormont argued.

"So be it!" Morgan answered. His soldiers unleashed all twelve boulders aiming them at Anius.

"Shields up now!" Anius commanded. He and his men huddled together with their shields over their heads. The faithful king looked up at the boulders coming toward them. He knew the impact would kill them all. He closed his eyes, prayed, and believed. The sound of the boulders' impact hurt the ears of Morgan, Dormont, and their men. That did not stop them from cheering for their victory. All they could see was smoke where Anius and his men once stood.

"I told you not to doubt Lucifer's power," Morgan said smugly.

"Anius and his men fought well but thanks to Lucifer and his deadly weapons, they never had a chance," Dormont boasted.

As the smoke cleared, Dormont noticed a blue glow appearing. Anius had shielded his army with heaven's flame. Dormont was horrified to see them all still alive.

"What? How?" Aries asked shocked. He could not believe that they were all still living. Anius' blue flame distinguished as he collapsed.

"That, Aries, was a gift from God," Xander answered Aries as he checked on his brother.

"I am alright but that took a lot of energy. We will not survive another hit," Anius answered, breathing heavily. He could not stand. "Tell the men to fall back. Send in . . . the cavalry," Anius said to Xander.

"Fall back!" Xander ordered the men as he and Aries helped Anius stand. "Cavalry, attack!" Xander shouted. Anius' cavalry rode in with haste from the castle entrance surprising Dormont and his brother. Morgan ordered the men to readjust the aim of their death machines to hit Anius and his men as they retreated.

"Light them up," Morgan ordered. His soldiers poured coal tar on the boulders, then lit them on fire.

"Infantry, protect the king!" Xander shouted. The soldiers huddled around Anius with their shields up ready to die for their king. This time, the boulders hit hard destroying all of Anius' army including his cavalry. All of his men were on fire. Again Morgan, Dormont, and their men cheered. They watched the large blaze proud of their work. More than half of their men were lost but Morgan felt that the casualties were worth it for this victory. Morgan and Dormont faced their men to thank them.

"You have all fought valiantly and should be proud, but our work is not done," Morgan shouted thrusting his sword in the air proudly.

"The queen is not to be harmed. Leave no one else standing. Take whatever you want, this castle is ours now. *This kingdom is ours!*" Dormont shouted. This time, he and his brother were the only ones cheering.

"M-m-my king!" His fearful soldier quivered as he pointed his finger toward the spot where Anius and his men were.

Dormont and his brother slowly turned around. All of Anius' men, including his brother, were dead, but Anius still stood ignited with his blue flame. He tried to protect his men but was not strong enough; the flame could only spare him this time. Anius looked down at his brothers' burning body, then let out a bloodcurdling scream.

"How does he still live? Lucifer said that we would conquer him," Morgan asked in disbelief. Dormont could not answer. As they all looked on, they saw the fire from the boulders that hit Anius and his men starting to slowly move away from them. The flame took the form of a person and was now gone. Only a small bit of it remained in someone's hand—that of Danara. She threw the fireball from her hand toward Lucifer's death machines destroying every last boulder.

"Come forward, cowards!" Danara ordered Dormont, Morgan, and their army. They walked toward her unable to control their own bodies. Anius was so filled with rage that he did not object to his wife's presence. He felt completely exhausted, but his anger for the death of his brother and faithful soldiers consumed him.

"That is far enough!" she commanded them as Karo joined her side.

"I should have known you would come to save your king, witch," Dormont teased.

"My king did not need saving. As you can see, he still stands," she answered. "Even as you stare death in the face, you still do not know how to mind your manners. Now, what shall we do about that?" Danara pondered. "Morgan. I order you to cut out your brother's tongue."

"*No!* Please," Morgan pleaded. He tried with all his will to stop himself but he saw the flames of hell in her eyes and had no choice but to obey.

"Morgan, I am your brother. Do not do this! Resist her!" Dormont pleaded unable to move. Anius took pleasure in hearing him scream as he watched Morgan use his brother's own sword to cut out his tongue. Dormont fell down on the ground wailing in pain. Anius took his place beside his queen.

"You kept your word. I am safe. Let me handle the rest, my love," she whispered to Anius. He was silent. She too was heartbroken from all of their soldiers' deaths.

Anius ignored her plea. He was in shock. His brother was gone. He watched him burn. All he could hear now was his own heart racing. Anius dropped his ax, removed his two swords from their holster, then attacked Dormont and Morgan's army relentlessly. He left Morgan frozen in fear saving him for last, then tore through his army as a man possessed. The men fought back hard but Anius' rage made him victorious every single time. Danara and Karo were stunned by his actions. She had known Anius since she was a child and always knew him to be determined, but this surprised her. She looked on impressed as Anius destroyed half of what remained of the enemies' army before he even felt winded. One of the soldiers took advantage when Anius finally slowed down and plunged his sword into his back. Anius barely felt the pain. He turned, then stuck both of his swords through each of the soldier's eyes and quickly sliced the throat of another close by. Danara and Karo began to attack. She drained the blood of as many as she could gathering energy for what was to come next. The three of them destroyed the remaining soldiers. When they were done, Anius fell to the ground. His energy was depleted. Karo immediately aided him. Danara stood in the center of both dead armies. She raised both of her arms pointing each one toward an army. She closed her eyes and tried to will the souls of Dormont and Morgan's army to rise. There were hundreds of dead soldiers all around her.

"Danara, don't!" Anius shouted. He understood what she was attempting and sensed that she was not strong enough. He could feel that the child she carried was in distress.

"*I command your souls to rise!*" she shouted at the dead soldiers. Blood began to pour out of her eyes, ears, and nose.

"Stop this at once! You are killing my child." She heard Lucifer speak. She looked down at the fallen soldiers' shields and swords, then saw Lucifer's reflection staring back at her.

"You've taken enough from me. You cannot have my family," she answered, then continued.

"How bold of you to think that you can take souls this way. Karo was different, he willingly gave you his soul. These soldiers did not. They are gone. You do not have a claim on them," Lucifer said.

"I have every right to claim them. Alexander and my army died defending me because of your efforts. You tried to break me but instead, you have unleashed me," Danara said sternly, then continued her work.

"Stop this now and I will no longer attack your family," Lucifer promised.

"The word of the father of lies has no value," she said, then began to choke on her own blood as it poured out of her mouth. Karo helped Anius going to her but neither of them could touch her. Something unseen prevented it. She could not be stopped.

"You are more powerful than they know, child," she said feeling terrible pain in her chest.

"I can feel your power surging through my body. Unleash it, or else we will both perish," Danara said clutching her stomach. Upon uttering the words, the enemies' dead bodies began to twitch. Their souls emerged, then entered Danara's body. She instantly felt energized.

"My loyal soldiers, you gave your life for me and in return, I will gladly sacrifice mine to restore you. *Return to me now*!" she commanded Xander and her dead army. The boulders that had crushed them vanished. Their skin and flesh were now restored. Their bodies arose from the ground and all eyes opened at once. The soldiers stared at each other in disbelief. They knew that she had brought them all back from death. They all bowed and bent their knees in honor of their queen. Anius was now able to touch her. He picked her up and held her drained body in his arms.

"You could have died," he whispered clutching her.

"They did die . . . Alexander died for me. I had to bring them back," she whispered faintly.

"Thank you so much for returning all of my brothers to me," he said, then kissed her gently. "Now please, promise me that you will never put your life in danger again." She did not answer. Her eyes were closed. Anius shook her thinking that she was gone. She opened her eyes, barely.

"I feel so cold," she said faintly.

"Take her inside," he ordered Karo. Karo immediately obeyed and took her back to the castle. Anius mounted a nearby horse. He too was exhausted and needed to speedily return to the castle to be by his love's side. He was pleased to see his brother and soldiers alive again.

"God allowed her to restore all except my chariot warriors," Anius looked to the sky.

"I am sorry, brother," Xander said sincerely. Anius smiled.

"I am not sorry. They earned their place in heaven. I will see them again one day," Anius said believing this with all of his heart.

"As for them, finish this!" Anius ordered. Aries picked up his ax from the ground while Xander got his war hammer. Anius rode off with haste. His infantry followed. Once he and Danara were gone, Lucifer's reflection disappeared.

"How fortunate we are that you two have been saved for last," Xander teased Morgan. Before he could respond, Aries raised his large ax, then struck Morgan down the middle of his body splitting him in two.

"Words cannot express how good that felt. I must come around more often. You royals sure know how to party." Aries laughed so hard it made his large belly ache. Xander laughed until something on the ground caught his eye.

"Oh, now I see why you are so quiet. Looks like you have lost your tongue." Xander chuckled as Dormont tried to beg for his life.

"I wonder what he is trying to say," Xander joked causing him and Aries to burst into laughter again.

"Okay, listen. I am not a monster. I will spare your life if you can simply say the words, I'm sorry," Xander said leaning over Dormont.

"Silly me, I have forgotten that you no longer have a tongue." Xander laughed, then suddenly a coldness came over him.

"This is for my queen!" he said raising his mighty war hammer, then slamming it onto Dormont's face repeatedly until his head was shattered. The soldiers gathered their weapons and shields, then made it back to the castle. Xander took one last look at the battlefield. There was nothing left but an empty field. All of the dead bodies were gone as if nothing had happened. Aries tapped him on the shoulder.

"There may be no evidence left of what happened, but we know it did. You fought well, my friend," Aries said proudly.

"You did as well, thank you for defending my family." Xander truly appreciated his loyalty.

"Always, until death," Aries replied, then they both laughed. "The things that I have witnessed and experienced today have shown me that the devil does exist and there is a God out there watching over us. I was not a believer before this day. From this day forth, I will never forget his mercy. God has made a believer out of me."

"He has made one out of me as well," Xander concluded as they walked inside to check on the king and queen.

"How is our queen?" Aries asked his king as he got patched up.

"She is resting," he answered.

"And you, my king?"

"I will be fine. Thank you Aries, both of you. We are so thankful for your loyalty and sacrifice," Anius said shaking his hand. "The queen has expressed that she would like for you to join our royal court," Anius said in full agreement of his wife's decision. Aries was overjoyed but maintained his composure. It was a high honor to be a part of the royal court; he knew his wife would be so pleased.

"Karo and some of my men will escort you home to retrieve your family. I would prefer to be cautious and make sure you are all safe. Who knows if Morgan and Dormont set things in motion once you denied them?" the king said.

"That is most generous, my king. My family and I are truly honored." Aries bowed.

"You certainly deserve it. I will accompany you. I am heading that way to take my mother home. She cannot handle all the excitement that goes on around here. She's confused enough as it is at her old age." Xander chuckled.

"You are terrible, brother. I will let Mother know you said that," Anius teased. "Thank God for our sister, she kept mother calm through everything and convinced her to return home. It's safer for her there. Josephine will remain here for now."

"Alright then, everything is settled. We will leave shortly. I will return quickly as I can, brother," Xander said, then embraced his brother and left with Aries and Karo.

The next few days were peaceful in their kingdom. Danara kept her distance from Anius and the others, but he understood why. She felt overwhelmed with everything that had happened and just needed to process it all, but she did stay close to Josephine. She had always loved her dearly and cherished their friendship. She felt more comfortable around her than anyone since she became pregnant. She had Josephine sleep next to her in her quarters the night before, but when she awakened the next morning, Danara was gone. Josephine had her maidens help her get dressed, then had breakfast with her brother. After breakfast, Anius went to his daily training with his men. Josephine searched the castle for Danara but she was nowhere to be found. Her search led her to the maze garden. She had been in this maze so many times she knew it like the back of her hand. Strangely, this time, she was lost. Every turn seemed like the bushes were closing in on her. She saw a light at the end of the bushes in front of her so she ran toward it. When she reached it, there were no more bushes—only a large, rusty door that she had never seen before. The door glowed.

"Fear not, Josephine. If the doorway has revealed itself to you, that means it is time and you are ready," Danara said suddenly appearing.

"Danara, you startled me. I was looking all over for you. What is this door?" Josephine asked inspecting it.

"Enter the doorway and find out," Danara said and kissed her hands, "Be strong, sister, and thank you."

"Be strong for what? Danara, I do not understand," Josephine said confused. Danara leaned forward.

"Thank you for the sacrifice that you are about to make," Danara whispered, then instantly, the door opened. Josephine felt her body levitate off the ground. She floated into the darkness.

"Wait! What is happening?" Josephine shouted as Danara's image kept getting smaller the deeper she floated into the darkness until everything went completely black.

Josephine lost consciousness when she went into the darkness. She could feel her body lying flat on the ground beneath her. She opened her eyes and saw a light so bright it hurt her eyes at first.

"Claudine, is that you?" Josephine asked once her eyes adjusted. She saw that she was in a bright room with Danara's three aunts Claudia, Claudette, and Claudine.

"How are you here? You died. I went to your funeral. Wait a minute. Am I dead?" Josephine asked now worried.

"Calm yourself, you are not dead," Claudine said helping her stand.

"Our earthly bodies died but our souls are bound here until—" Claudia paused.

"Until what?" Josephine asked.

"Until our purpose is fulfilled," Claudette answered.

"You have a purpose as well Josephine and it is of the utmost importance," said Claudine.

"I mean no offense but I think you are mistaken. What purpose could I possibly have? I'm nothing, no one. I cannot even find a husband," she said sadly, "I married once again after King Thoron, but when I did not produce an heir, he annulled our marriage," Josephine said almost in tears. She had not spoken of this in some time but the pain was still there.

"Stop feeling sorry for yourself," Claudia said sternly.

"Claudia!" Her sister Claudette scolded her, shaking her head. Claudia was always the toughest of her sisters. She rarely had sympathy for anyone and always chose to get straight to the point.

"We do not have time for this," Claudia answered annoyed. "You know about the horrible things Danara has gone through and that your brother has chosen to stand by her and protect the unborn child," Claudia began.

"Yes. I am so sorry for what happened to your niece. I will help her in any way that she needs," Josephine answered truthfully.

"Our niece does not need your pity. She will need your strength and so will the child," Claudia said bluntly. Josephine did not know what to say.

"Get down on your knees," Claudia demanded. Josephine glanced at Claudine and Claudette who said nothing. She got down on her knees. The three sisters gathered and stood in front of her with Claudia in the middle.

"Your faith in God is strong," Claudette said touching Josephine's right shoulder.

"You will need it," Claudine said holding onto her left shoulder.

"Is your faith strong enough to withstand what is ahead?" Claudia asked, then placed her hand on Josephine's head. The sisters' heads then merged into one. Josephine could not believe her own eyes. Their bodies remained and their hands were still touching her but there was now one large head connecting them. It had only one large slanted eye that was closed. Josephine was frightened of it and she had good reason to be. Once the eye slowly opened, it revealed horrific images from the past, present, and future. When the images stopped, Josephine fell to her side vomiting. The sisters' bodies returned back to normal. Claudette and Claudine went to help her.

"Now you know all you need to make a decision," Claudia said sternly.

"But there . . . there was so much blood and death," Josephine said still in shock as her body trembled.

"There was also light and love, but before that, there is always pain and suffering. For it is through pain that we truly understand love and unlock our true potential. Are you ready to unlock yours?" Claudia asked.

"Will you make the same choice as you brother?" Claudine asked.

"Do you understand what it is that we are asking?" Claudette asked. Josephine wiped her tears, then stood up.

"*Yes!*" she answered with conviction. Claudia stared into her eyes and studied her. She saw that Josephine's heart was true.

"Thank you for your loyalty. Now, let your training begin." Claudia smiled.

"Training?" Josephine asked.

"Yes, training. Your brother was given heaven's flame by God's Phoenix but you, Josephine, will have an entirely different experience," Claudia began.

"My sisters and I were born with powerful spiritual gifts. We have always been able to see the future. You were born with natural abilities that you have not yet unlocked because it was not time. Now is the time, you must believe it," Claudia said, then a large rectangular mass of water appeared behind her. "Step inside," she insisted.

"You want me to step inside of that water? Why? What is going to happen to me?" Josephine asked afraid.

"Trust us, child. Step inside," Claudette said calmly, then walked her over to the water. Josephine placed a finger inside of the water. It was cold but there was nothing odd about it. It was actual water.

"Is this truly necessary?" Josephine asked.

"This is the only way you can help Danara. You will understand more once you step inside," Claudette reassured her. Josephine took one step closer to the massive wall of water, then it sucked her in. She panicked and tried to get out but could not.

"You are an elemental. One of the strongest we've ever met," Claudia said circling her. "You have the power to control the water, but you must find the strength within you to do so."

Josephine panicked as water began to fill her lungs. She could not comprehend why they would not help her. Her heartbeat began to slow down as she gasped for air knowing it was too late. Death was inevitable. She took her final breath as she prayed, then drowned to death.

"There you go. Let it out." Josephine heard Claudette say as she patted her back and she coughed up water.

"What happened?" Josephine asked puzzled.

"You failed, so you died," Claudia answered disappointed. "Get her up," Claudia demanded as she manifested the wall of water again. Her sisters obeyed.

"Wait! Why are you doing this? I said I would help Danara, I do not understand," Josephine pleaded.

"How can you help her fight the evil that hunts her and her child? You are not yet ready. We are teaching you, preparing you. You have the power to wield this water. Doubt is what holds you back. Until you wield it, we will do this over and over," Claudia said without emotion. "Now try again," she demanded.

"Wait just a moment," Josephine begged. Claudia willed Josephine's body back into the water. The sisters watched as she struggled once more until the water drowned her again. When she regained consciousness, Claudia was standing over her.

"Again!" Claudia ordered immediately not even giving her time to catch her breath.

Josephine was trapped again in the water wall. This time, she was filled with anger. She was angry with Claudia for being so merciless—angry about the pain in her lungs that felt like they would explode. She thought of the horrible visions the three sisters showed her. Instead of fighting to breathe, she remained still and focused.

"God, I have always been your loyal servant. If this power truly exists in me, please help me to control it. Use me as your instrument to do your will. I surrender to you," she prayed as her lungs filled with water. She suddenly felt the water push out of her lungs as she started to believe that she could conquer this. The water began to freeze all around her. The sisters watched amazed.

"What is happening?" Claudine asked.

"She believes," Claudia answered proudly. The water was now completely frozen. The sisters heard a cracking sound, then the entire wall shattered and Josephine's body floated in the air. She slowly landed on her feet. She felt an energy surge through her.

"You did it!" Claudine and Claudette said in unison.

"Yes, well, it only took her about twenty times." Claudia pretended to be unimpressed. "Now it's time for your next trial."

"But I did what you asked," Josephine said.

"There is much you must learn. Now, you must burn," Claudia said. Although Claudia was not one to joke around, Josephine thought that she was kidding until she was surrounded by fire.

"Please, stop. I do not want to burn," Josephine pleaded.

"Then wield it. Now you believe the power is in you, control the element or die," Claudia said as the fire began to burn Josephine's legs. She screamed in agony. Claudine and Claudette looked away. They felt terrible for what she was going through but they knew it was necessary. Josephine's body quickly burned until there was nothing left of her.

Once again, the sisters brought her back to life. Her body was naked and completely burned. She could barely move.

"I know how you feel. You are hurting and tired, but you must learn to control your power. This is the only way," Claudia said, then set her body on fire again. Josephine's powerful scream shook the room.

"*Enough! I control you!*" she screamed, then a flood of water came out of her mouth immediately extinguishing the fire. All three sisters were impressed.

"Now, you are getting it," Claudia said sounding almost proud. "How do you feel?" she asked.

"Like I am still on fire," Josephine answered as Claudette put a robe on her.

"Then allow me to cool you down," Claudine said manifesting a large gust of wind from her hands so powerful it threw Josephine against the wall shattering her spine. She could not stand. The wind was so strong it began to tear away her skin exposing her flesh and bone. She felt like she was being punished when all she wanted to do was help.

*I can't do this. I am weak. I am nothing*, she thought to herself. She felt so defeated.

"Get up, Josephine," she heard Danara's voice in her head cheering her on. "I need you to master this. I'm so sorry you are suffering but I know you, I believe in you, my sister. Now get up," Danara said tenderly.

"I . . . I can't, my spine is broken," Josephine cried.

"'I can't' are the words of a quitter, that is not who you are. God only chooses those who believe they can, those who have the will, those who know Jesus Christ is their strength. God does not choose wrong. The Lord is with you and he suffered more than you are suffering right now when he died on the cross for your sins. If you truly believe the lies of Lucifer when he tells you that you are worthless and weak, if you trust his words over God's, then I do not know you at all. I lost faith in God and he still used me to resurrect your brother. You have never lost faith, what do you think God would do for you? Call upon the Lord, ask him to lift you up with your broken spine, believe in him, and I promise you he will," Danara said with all certainty. Josephine could no longer hear her voice. She tried again to stand but still could not.

"Lord Jesus, I trust and believe in you. I humbly ask you to please lift me up!" she shouted, then willed the wind to raise her off of the ground. She trusted in God, believed in Jesus, and he delivered her giving her exactly what she needed to conquer her doubts and fears. He gave her the power to not only wield the elements but also the power to do whatever her mind could conceive.

"That is exactly what I wanted to see. You are almost ready," Claudia said pretending to be unimpressed.

"Almost? You are mistaken. The Lord Jesus says that I am ready," Josephine said, then willed the wind into a form of a tornado that swallowed Claudia.

"Josephine, release her!" Claudine and Claudette begged, then tried to use their power to destroy the tornado but they could not.

"I do not wish to hurt her," Josephine said, then willed the tornado to safely release Claudia which then disappeared. "I just needed her to understand that I can protect the family now. If God says that I am ready, then who is Claudia to tell me that I am not? She no longer hears his voice because of her own jealousy but you two can still hear him, so tell her what she already knows," Josephine spoke with a renewed confidence. Her tone was different; her very demeanor was not the same as it was before. When she first came to them, she was weak. The sisters knew now that not only was she strong but she was also blessed by Jesus Christ. They were seers yet did not foresee this. They knew now that she had a calling even higher than they expected. God instructed them to teach her, then he elevated her higher than any elemental that came before her.

"She is right. God says that she is ready," the sisters said in unison.

"Forgive me. I felt the power in you greater than my own and I did feel jealousy when I should have been thankful. You are ready and since it was the Lord himself that blessed you, I believe you will protect this family and do what he has entrusted you to do," Claudia said with great humility. There was nothing else that the sisters could teach so they bowed, then hugged Josephine. A bright light surrounded her.

"Thank you for believing in me when I didn't," Josephine said tearfully.

"We knew that you could do it. Remember we see all. When you need our guidance, we will be here. Now go, and keep our loved ones safe." Claudia hugged her. Josephine felt tired as the light around her got brighter, then sent her home.

"Princess Josephine," her maiden said waking her up. Josephine looked around realizing she was in her quarters laying down on her bed.

"The king and queen have requested that you join them in court," the maiden said.

"Very well. Was I asleep for long? I was just in the garden, wasn't I?" she asked sitting up.

"You were in the garden your highness, then you said you were tired and wanted to rest. Shall I bring your food and tell them you are not well?" her maiden asked.

"No, I am just fine. I will join them shortly," Josephine answered, then her maiden left. She thought everything that happened was a dream until she walked by the fireplace on her way out, then willed the fire with her mind to extinguish. The fire obeyed and quickly went out. Josephine smiled to herself, then went to court.

She entered the massive hall now full of their royal subjects. This was the part of being a royal that she hated. People always have something to complain about and this was their opportunity.

"Come and sit by me, Josephine," Danara beamed. "I heard from my aunts that you did well. I had no doubt," Danara gently touched her hand.

"There is nothing that I wouldn't do for the family. Your words truly helped me, sister, thank you," Josephine answered sincerely.

"What are you two whispering about?" Xander asked taking a seat next to his sister. He had just returned with Karo and Aries' family but Aries was not with them.

"We will speak about it later. For now, let us hear what our people have to say," Danara said. Xander questioned them no more.

"First off, we would like to welcome Aries and his family to court," Danara said, then everyone bowed and welcomed them.

"My king and queen, you are most kind. My family thanks you for all of your generosity," Aries' wife said bowing.

"Where is Aries?" Anius asked.

"He said he had business to attend to and will return shortly," she answered.

Suddenly, the hall doors opened with soldiers from the north entering.

"Forgive our intrusion. We have an urgent matter to discuss," one of the soldiers said as he pushed through the crowd with a prisoner bound by chains wearing an iron mask on his head.

"What is the meaning of this?" Anius asked. The soldiers removed the mask revealing Aries.

"My king and queen, Aries has committed treason. He has murdered the leaders of several kingdoms," the soldier said, then threw a large bag on the floor. The bag was covered in blood filled with human heads.

"Oh, dear God!" Aries' wife gasped. She knew that for this offense, they could all be killed.

"Aries, explain yourself," Danara demanded.

"My queen. These are the heads of all who wronged you. They did Morgan and Dormont's bidding. These traitors deserved to die for dishonoring you," Aries answered.

The soldiers placed each head on the ground for all to see. Danara recognized the faces of all who said she was the devil's whore. The only head missing was Princess Margot's. She knew it was not in Aries to harm a woman, especially one who was pregnant.

"He had no right to take these lives. He should be hung for treason," the soldier suggested. Danara stood up.

"Right? What do you know of right? Aries is now leader of my royal guard. Those people dishonored me. They are the ones who committed treason. Aries restored my honor and for that, I am grateful. Now, release him," she commanded.

"But my queen, our . . ." the soldier began. Danara did not want to hear what he had to say.

"I will not repeat myself," she said coldly. The soldiers immediately released Aries from the chains that bound him.

"Take your place beside your king, Aries," she said and he quickly obeyed.

"If you feel that Aries was wrong, then, by all means, exact your revenge. Understand that any retaliation against him will make you an enemy of the kingdom and we will not stand for it," she said now feeling uneasy. She could feel the anger rising in her own people toward her. They did not all agree with Aries' actions. She heard all of their thoughts and felt hate growing in their hearts. One of her court members known as Simon Norah stared at her with disapproving eyes. When he saw that she noticed his disapproval, he faked a smile, then looked away. Danara picked up one of the heads from the ground.

"You knew this one," she said holding the head of a dead duke in front of Simon Norah.

"This was your cousin. Do you wish to join him?" she asked with no emotion. All were afraid.

"My. . . my loyalty is only to you," Simon Norah pleaded.

"If your actions do not align with your words, then you will suffer worse," she said placing the head of his cousin into his hands.

"Whatever I have done to offend you, I am deeply sorry, your highness," he continued to beg.

"Silence!" Danara insisted, then took her seat.

"As you can see, we have no tolerance for those that question our rule." Anius stood up addressing the soldier that brought Aries.

"My king, I apologize. I am acting as I was ordered, too. Aries' actions angered many. More will come and they will want answers," he answered afraid. Anius calmly took the head from Simon Norah and handed it to the soldier.

"Let them come. They are more than welcome. As for you, leave our sight immediately before it is you that loses your head next," Anius said firmly.

"Brother, you just made me proud. You know I like it when you talk like that," Xander said after Anius returned to his seat.

"My love should always feel protected and supported," Anius said kissing his wife's hand. She did not pull away from him nor seem annoyed. She looked at him lovingly the way she used to.

"Does anyone else have anything they would like to discuss?" Danara asked, then a young woman stepped forward.

"My queen, I bring good news from the East. Princess Margot has given birth to a healthy baby boy. Her father wishes to invite you all to celebrate his birth in a few weeks once she is better," the young maiden said. Danara immediately thought of how the princess also uttered those horrible words to her and wished Aries would have taken her head too.

"Well, that is wonderful news. Please let them know that we will all be in attendance for such a joyous occasion," Danara said as pleasantly as she could. She faked it well but Anius knew this was hard for her.

"Alright, this calls for a drink and some music. We must welcome and honor Aries and his family," Anius deflected standing and raising a glass, then everyone followed.

"To good health and great fortune. May our kingdom continue to thrive and long live our queen," he toasted.

"Long live the queen!" everyone repeated. The harps began to play and everyone danced. When Anius sat back down, Danara was gone.

"Where did she go?" he asked Xander and Josephine.

"I'm not sure. We should give her a moment. There is something I must tell you both," Josephine said as Aries walked away to join his family after thanking Anius for not letting them execute him.

"You will not believe this, but I just met with Danara's aunts Claudette, Claudine, and Claudia," Josephine said excitedly sharing her news.

"How is that possible? They died years ago," Xander stated.

"Nothing that happens around here seems to surprise me anymore." Anius smirked, then Josephine told them what had happened to her.

Danara paced in her bedroom full of anger. She thought to herself how unfair it was that Princess Margot gets to have her healthy normal baby while she had to suffer with the child of the devil himself growing inside of her.

*You are the devil's whore and you carry his child.* She kept hearing Princess Margot's voice in her head repeating the same words over and over. She knew that Princess Margot was left with an impossible choice yet this still enraged her. She tried to calm herself and return to the others but she wanted vengeance more. She opened her double patio doors and took a deep breath. She understood that Lucifer put these thoughts in her mind and that she should not act, but before she knew it, she was standing on the edge of her balcony looking down. She wanted to jump and end everything but she knew that she nor the child would die. There was only one thing that would soothe her now and that was blood. Danara let her feet go from the balcony, closed her eyes, then began to fall. Before she hit the ground, her body began to float upward. She floated around fascinated. The air felt so good on her skin. She flew higher and went wherever the wind took her. She ended up on another balcony and did not recognize the kingdom at first. She saw a figure asleep on their bed and walked through the door. The first thing she noticed was a child's crib with a baby in it and knew this was the home of Princess Margot. The baby smiled at her as Danara picked him up.

"You are a very handsome boy," she said, then kissed his tiny forehead. His mother instantly awoke. She saw someone holding her son.

"Who are you? Put my son down or I will call for my guards," she demanded. Danara walked into the light so she could see her face.

"Oh, my goodness! My queen, please forgive me, I did not know that it was you. No one informed me that you were coming," she apologized.

"He is a beautiful child. What do you call him?" Danara asked holding him gently. "Leonidas, named after his father. We have worked things out and will be married soon." She smiled awkwardly at her queen.

"How blessed you are. You'll have your husband and your beautiful son. What a great life you will have," Danara said. Princess Margot became weary of her queen's tone remembering what happened the last time she saw her.

"Can you please hand me my son, it is time for me to feed him," she said nervously.

"Margot, you sound afraid. What could you possibly have to be afraid of?" Danara smiled moving closer.

"It's just that I am so ashamed about what happened. I never should have said those words to you. It has troubled me terribly causing me to deliver my son early," she said sadly.

"Trust me, I understand the position you were in. You had to choose between being loyal to your queen or losing your son. He is perfect. You made a wise decision," Danara said still smiling.

"Did you know that Aries took the heads of everyone that betrayed me that day except yours? He did not have it in his heart to kill a pregnant woman," Danara said.

"I am so sorry. I will forever regret that day. Please tell me how to make it right," Margot begged.

"If you had to choose between your life or your son's life, what would you choose?" Danara asked rocking the baby.

"Please do not hurt my son," she cried, then dropped on her knees kissing Danara's feet. Danara willed Leonidas to float in the air just over his mother's head. She did not allow Margot to reach him.

"Please, you know I had no choice," Margot cried hysterically.

"I know, princess, but the pain you have caused me cannot go unpunished," Danara said grabbing her throat. Princess Margot, for your act of treason against your queen, I sentence you to death," Danara said squeezing her neck.

"Let me tell you a secret before you die." Danara pulled her closer. "I do carry Lucifer's child and he has given me immense power. Allow me to show you," she whispered, then placed her lips on Margot's, forcing her soul to emerge. She quickly consumed it, then tossed Margot's body aside and took Leonidas into her arms again.

"I am a little sorry that you had to witness that. I promise I will not harm you. Your life will be a long one and you will be very powerful. I promise you that for what I have taken from you," she vowed as he smiled at her. Danara kissed his cheek, then returned him to his crib. She left through the double doors quietly closing them behind her, then flew back to her kingdom so fast that no one noticed she was gone. She felt so full she immediately went to bed. Her baby was very satisfied with the soul she just took. Danara was satisfied with her revenge. That night, she finally slept peacefully without nightmares.

Xander grew weary in the weeks that followed. He saw a great change in Josephine. She quickly adapted to her new powers which gave her a lot of confidence. She no longer felt inadequate. Xander was happy for her but he felt useless. He died in the war against Dormont and Morgan and knew he was no match for Lucifer. He wished to yield some power of his own. This thought began to consume him and made him become jealous of his siblings. He now spent his days drunk and nights with women whose names he would forget the next day. It had been four and a half months since Lucifer took Danara's virginity and planted his seed inside of her womb. Xander was convinced that the child was evil. It was the devil's child and it changed everything that made Danara who she was. They all knew that she killed Princess Margot but no one discussed it. The old Danara never would have done such a thing. This new Danara murdered people daily. She said the child fed off of the souls she consumed but Anius knew that she also enjoyed it, and this made him become distant. He still kept a watchful eye on her but he had given up on their love. Xander felt sorry for his brother. He was very sorry that he liked the new Danara in a way that if his brother knew, he would probably kill him. He could not wait to see her beautiful face every morning after having passionate dreams of her almost every night. He lusted after her and thought it would drive him mad because he knew that he could never have her. He walked down the corridor on his way to breakfast thinking of how immaculate her curvaceous body was. It was early. The castle was quiet which was fine by him since he wanted to be alone with his thoughts. He was thinking of going to visit his mother and taking a break from everything. He knew his impure thoughts of Danara were wrong, forbidden. He walked into the dining hall and there she was.

"Good morning!" Danara said kissing him on each cheek. She looked like a dark goddess. Her hair was now black, her rosy cheeks were pale, and her lips were plumper than normal as well as her breast. An odd thing was her belly had not grown. Xander did not know much about the stages of pregnancy but he thought by now that she would be showing.

"You are up early. You're usually still drunk and asleep at this time." She giggled, then took his hand leading him to the dining room table. He pulled out her chair for her. She told him to sit beside her, then ordered her maiden to fetch him some breakfast. Xander gazed at her for a moment intoxicated by her beauty and scent. She smelled lovely. He wondered what her sweet familiar scent could be.

"Lilies," she said.

"What about lilies?" he asked.

"My scent is lilies. You look as though you just inhaled me," she joked.

"Forgive me, it's just as you said earlier. I am still drunk from last night," he lied and faked a smile. She smiled back; she had lied also. She knew exactly what he was thinking. She enjoyed reading his naughty thoughts about her. It was a game for her so she made sure to wear revealing clothes that showed off her body. At times, she would brush her body against his pretending it was innocent on her part because she knew it made him blush and feel uncomfortable at the same time. She did this especially because it angered Anius although he had not yet addressed it. As her pregnancy progressed, she couldn't bear to see his face most days and she did not care about his feelings. She blamed him for everything and sometimes, she was convinced that he was Lucifer. She wanted to kill him so instead, she would kill others, mostly her own people; not just to feed but to control the anger that burned inside of her.

"What are you having?" Xander interrupted her thoughts.

"Just a glass of wine and some fresh strawberries. I'm surprised there is any wine left with you around," she teased.

"The day we run out of wine is the day I leave you." He laughed.

"I would not be able to bear that." She touched his cheek.

"You would be fine. I am sure you would not even notice that I'm gone," he said sipping her wine.

"Don't say such a thing, you have been such a comfort. I wouldn't know what to do without you. Are you thinking of leaving?" she asked taking her wine glass from him, then pouring him one.

"Actually, the thought crossed my mind. I may go check on my mother and stay there for a while. You don't need me. I can't protect you anyway. You will be fine with my brother and sister," he answered.

"I will not have it nor will I let you speak of yourself as if you are useless. Please do not leave, Alexander. I need you. You take my mind off of things and"—she paused—"I am sorry, this is selfish of me. If you wish to go, you have every right." She looked away.

"No, I'm sorry. I hate to upset you or make you think of what happened. I feel so useless because I cannot protect you."

"Xander, you died protecting me. I can never thank you enough. You are far from useless. You are my hero. You fought and died on the battlefield like a true warrior. That is what you are. Never think differently." She touched his leg. This made him feel warm from his leg to his loins. He moved his chair closer to the table so she could not see the sudden growth in his pants.

"Thank you for your kind words. I promised to help you. I will keep my word. I would die for you all over again. Now, let's not speak of this anymore," he reassured her, then sipped his wine. "I am yours."

"You're mine?" she asked coyly.

"Yes. For as long as you want me."

Anius interrupted them when he walked in.

"Good morning," he said sitting beside Danara. The maidens brought in food for Anius and Xander.

"My apologies, I feel like I interrupted," Anius said uncomfortably.

"I was just telling Xander how unbearable it would be here if he left."

"Are you thinking of leaving us, brother?" Anius asked hoping he'd say yes. He loved his brother, but these past few months were hard. They had grown closer but he felt at times Danara may be using his brother as a pawn to hurt him.

"I was thinking of visiting Mother but Danara convinced me to stay," he said as Danara stood up and excused herself.

"I appreciate your commitment to the family. Maybe you should find yourself a wife. There are some good women here. I'm sure you know since you have bedded most of them," Anius teased.

"Ha! You know me better than that. I am not the marrying type."

"You just haven't found the right one," Anius answered.

"There is no such thing. Do enjoy your breakfast, brother. I need a bath. I had quite a few of the lovely women of your kingdom last night and I can assure you Mother would not have approved of any of them," Xander said grabbing the bottle of wine.

"You are shameful. Father would be proud." Anius shook his head.

"Agreed." Xander winked, then walked out. Anius returned to his quarters and prayed.

The maidens drew Xander a hot bath, then disrobed him. He was about to get into the bath when Danara walked in. He quickly hid his naked body.

"Don't let me interrupt you," she said unbothered by his nudity. Xander got into the bath. Danara watched as the maidens rubbed his back and shoulders with sponges.

"Leave us," she ordered. The maidens put their heads down and quickly left. Danara took one of the sponges and slowly scrubbed his back. Xander felt relaxed as she slowly ran the sponge on his neck and chest, then her hand disappeared in the water as she reached his erect penis then gently rubbed it with her hand as Xander moaned.

"Danara, please stop," he said but he did not mean it.

"Do you really want me too?" she whispered as her lips gently touched his ears. He did not answer.

"I know how you truly feel about me, Xander. You cannot hide it," she whispered stroking his penis faster.

"I know you are in love with me. That is why I must ask something of you that I know you and only you can do. When the child is born, you must kill it," she continued.

"D-Danara I cannot," he said trying to move her hand but she was in full control. She roughly grabbed his hair pulling his head back while she stroked him faster.

"You will do this for me if you truly love me. You know this child is evil and will destroy this world. Anius and Josephine's minds are clouded but not yours. You are stronger and smarter than they are."

"I am not stronger. I do not have any power," Xander said feeling like he was going to explode.

"Promise me this and I will give you all that you desire," she insisted.

"Yes . . . yes I swear it. I will do it. I promise," he said as he closed his eyes and finally climaxed. His body felt weak and satisfied in a way he hadn't felt with any woman. He looked up and she was gone. The maidens returned and cleaned him.

Danara went to her favorite place, the garden of lilies, to ease her mind. She knew that what she had just done was wrong. She betrayed her husband and their vows. A part of her knew this was wrong while the evil part of her that was completely taking over was content with her actions, and was confident that Xander would do what she asked.

"So, here you are!" Josephine said sitting beside her on the stone bench.

"Why are you always following me?" Danara asked agitated.

"I have to keep you safe, even from yourself. I know what you are doing," Josephine said firmly.

"Not that I care but what exactly are you referring to?" Danara asked.

"You are playing a dangerous game with my brothers," Josephine stated.

"Oh, I see, now that you have power, you suddenly know it all." Danara smirked.

"I know enough. I see the way Xander looks at you and so does your husband. Anius does not deserve the pain you continue to inflict on him," Josephine said fed up. Danara got up from the bench.

"Do you honestly think that I care? There is no love left inside of me, only darkness," she said as Josephine searched her soul and felt only emptiness.

"There is still a part of you that cares. You were happy when I did the trials. I endured that for you and our family. You know what is to come," she pleaded.

"I was different then and I knew that it was necessary for you to go through the metamorphosis. I've seen glimpses of the future but I know something that you do not," she said coyly.

"What is that, sister?"

"The future you and I saw is not definite. It can be altered. If the child dies, then all that you saw will change," Danara answered.

"It is God himself that for his own reasons wants this child to live. No one can go against his will. That is why we have all been brought together."

"*God!*" Danara screamed. "I am so tired of hearing about God. All that we have been taught about him is not true. God turned his back on me long ago. The abomination growing inside my womb is proof of that. Where was God when that monster forced himself inside of me? Where was God when Lucifer tore me inside out and made me watch my mother die?" Danara cried. Josephine was brought to tears.

"Sister, I am so incredibly sorry for what Lucifer did to you. Please trust me when I say that God is with you now and always. You may no longer trust or believe in him but he will never forsake you," Josephine said sincerely. Danara turned away from her. Josephine could hear Danara's heart beating fast. She placed her hand on her shoulder. Danara turned around and faced her. Her eyes were black, her teeth became fangs, and her nails were now long black claws. She no longer looked human.

"*There is no God!*" she shouted into Josephine's face frightening her to her core. For a moment, she thought Danara would kill her, but in an instant, she took off into the sky out of her sight. She stood there frozen, still afraid. She felt like she had just seen the face of the devil himself. She gathered herself, then ran into the castle to alert the others. They searched vigilantly for her. Danara was nowhere to be found. She returned in a few hours as if nothing happened.

"Danara, where have you been? We searched everywhere for you," Anius said following her as she walked to her quarters.

"I am free to come and go as I please. I can protect myself. I do not need you all hovering over me constantly," she shouted.

"We're all just concerned," Anius said calmly.

"Well, as you can see, I am fine!" she shouted slamming her bedroom door in his face.

"Anius, the guards said that she returned," Josephine said running over to him. "How is she?"

"The same as she always is. *Angry!*" he said walking away.

It wasn't until two days later that they found out Danara had slaughtered a nearby village when she went missing. She felt no remorse for killing her own people. Anius and the others could not control her rage nor satisfy her hunger. Anius found her to be so intolerable that he no longer spoke to her. However, he still remained close not just for her safety but to also keep their people safe from her. This was impossible with her powers growing. His powers grew as well. Wherever she went, he could always find her and he would find the butchered corpses of their own people as well. This broke his heart. He begged God every day to have mercy on them all and to be his strength for he could not take this anymore. He became consumed with grief. Every day, his people would come begging for help to find their missing family members or friends that Danara killed. The kingdom was in fear, but their king could not save them. He grew sadder every day until he became sick with a fever. No one could heal him so they began to fear for his life after he burned for three days with no change. Danara did not care and had not gone to see him. His sickness made things better for her because now she could come and go as she pleased and he was too sick to get out of bed and find her. Josephine and the royal physician cared for him as best as they could but she knew he needed Danara. She pleaded with her to see him but to no avail.

"I think it's time that we sent for mother," Josephine said to Xander as they watched their brother sleep.

"I know what you are thinking. He is not going to die," Xander replied sternly.

"Mother has the right to say goodbye to her son. The doctor and I have done all that we can," she answered holding back tears.

"Danara can help him. She saved me and the army, she can do the same for him," Xander said full of hope.

"She was not as monstrous then as she is now. She does not care if her own husband lives or dies. Maybe you should ask her. She certainly seems to favor you more than her husband these days." Josephine gave him a look of disgust, then placed a fresh cold cloth on Anius' forehead.

"What is that supposed to mean?" he responded with anger.

"You know exactly what it means. You're in love with her. It is written all over your face whenever her name is mentioned or she enters the room," she answered as she continued to care for their brother.

"How dare you. She is our brother's wife!"

"Yes. She is his wife yet your heart still longs for her. The sad thing is that you think she feels the same way, but Danara doesn't love anyone. You'd be smart to remember that," she said giving an empty water pitcher to one of the maidens to fetch fresh water for the king.

"Josephine, I would never betray our brother. I am not in love with her," he lied.

"*Leave!*" she shouted annoyed.

"You have no right—" he began but she interrupted him.

"I know the next words you say will be lies and I will not entertain them. Make yourself useful and go convince her to save our brother," she scolded him.

"I do not know where she is nor think she will even listen to me," he answered.

"The fact that you are still standing here speaks volumes. You would definitely benefit if our brother died. I'm sure you would take his queen and become king yourself so I understand your apprehension. You disgust me. I can assure you if he dies, we are all doomed. This is not a part of God's plan. This is Lucifer's doing. He is even working through you right now or else you would stop at nothing to save our brother as he would do for you."

Xander felt struck by her words. They hurt him deeply because they were true. He was so ashamed of himself that he could not respond.

"Just go." She pointed at the door.

"I will find a way to save him. I promise you," he finally spoke, then quickly left the room in search of Danara. He found her in her bedroom on the balcony.

"Is there anything you can do for him?" Xander asked.

"I raised you from the dead, didn't I?" she replied smugly.

"Danara, please!" he pleaded.

"Have you ever felt trapped, Alexander?" she asked looking at the view of her kingdom. He did not respond in fear of saying the wrong thing.

"No matter how far away I go, I always end up back here. I am cursed by God and Lucifer. I think that possibly the curse will be lifted once your brother is dead." Her sinister smile sent chills down his spine.

"How could you stand by and let him die after everything he's done for you? He's been completely devoted to you even though you hate him. He loves you."

"You love me. Do you think he knows that? I wonder how crushed he would be if he knew. Maybe he does and that contributed to his illness." She chuckled. Xander's heartbeat quickened. He felt so much fear at this moment. She was now pure evil.

"You are right to fear me. I barely ate today and I am getting hungry." She licked her lips. Xander realized she was reading his every thought. He was so afraid especially knowing there was no way of stopping her if she wanted to tear him to shreds.

"Danara, I beg you, please save my brother." He continued to plead but she did not care. She just sipped her wine staring into the distance.

"I know that you hate him but it was not my brother that wronged you. Please heal him. I promised to kill Lucifer's child but if you let Anius die . . . I will not honor that promise," he said angering her. She dropped her glass, then swiftly grabbed him by the throat with such strength that his feet left the ground.

"You just made a big mistake," she snarled.

"Danara, wait!" She heard Josephine shout from the balcony across from them. She had heard the commotion while she was caring for Anius.

"Please, I cannot lose them both," Josephine begged.

"You better honor our fucking agreement," Danara said, then quickly switched places with Josephine. She moved so fast that before Xander hit the ground, Josephine was already beside him and Danara was on the opposite balcony. They watched her walk into Anius' bedroom, then close the double doors. His room was so quiet she could not hear his heartbeat and thought he was dead. She sat down on the bed beside him, then closed her eyes and touched his face. She slowly ran her fingers over his eyes, then his nose and lips.

"You do not deserve to suffer like this," she said placing her hand over his heart. It was still beating. As much as she'd recently changed, she could not deny that a part of her still felt connected to him. She still loved him even though she wouldn't admit that to him or anyone else.

"I did not think that you would come," Anius said weakly.

"I see you still think you know it all," she said gently rubbing a cold cloth on his face and chest. He burned with fever.

"You have been murdering your own people who love and adore you. Have you come to claim my soul as well?" He coughed up blood.

"What is happening to you?" she asked concerned. At that moment, she knew that he was dying and she fought with the decision to let him live or die. Her heart was torn. The evil that flowed through her veins had also poisoned her mind but her heart still belonged to Anius.

"I . . . I am sorry. I did this to you," she said truthfully. She could feel his pain, his sorrow, and although he was disgusted with who she'd become, she could still feel his love for her.

"Finish what you came to do, Angel of Death," Anius said as blood secreted from his nose.

"You think I came to kill you? I thought you believed your God would not allow it. You haven't fulfilled your promise yet," she mocked him.

"I know that you no longer believe in him but I always will, no matter what happens to me. If God has chosen to end my suffering, I welcome it." His words struck her like an arrow piercing her heart. He would rather die than be in her life. This made her heartache. She completely understood that she drove him to feel that way. It hurt her to see how badly she broke him down. He was once a man whose honor meant everything to him. He loved her and his family with all of his heart but she broke it and now, she regretted this deeply. She placed his left hand on her stomach and her right hand over his heart. Anius felt the heat radiating from her belly as his health slowly improved. He also felt movement in her womb. Danara stood up immediately after he was fully restored.

"Are you alright?" he asked concerned about her not even realizing he was now completely healed and standing before her. She did not respond. He helped her sit down, then sat beside her.

"Thank you for healing me. I know it must've taken a lot of energy. You should rest," he said worried about her.

"No, it's not that. It . . . it moved. The child moved for the first time when I placed your hand on my stomach," she said surprised.

"I felt it too," Anius said. Danara put his hand on her stomach again, then closed her eyes. "Your touch has quieted all the noise in my head. The child favors you. For a moment you've given me"— she stopped and took a deep breath relishing the feeling—"you have given me peace." Her voice trembled, then she exhaled.

"Can I lay with you?" she asked not wanting this peaceful feeling to end.

"Of course, anything for you." He was relieved not only because he was no longer ill but also for being able to give her some peace. He laid down behind her. She gripped his hand tight on her stomach. She laid comfortably in the arms of the man who truly loved her unconditionally. She had treated him horribly, slaughtered most of their kingdom, yet here he was extending his love to a child that was not his not just for God but also because he loved her that much. She now believed they were all united for a reason. Only his great love could get her through this and what his family was doing for her, she could never repay.

"Thank you, Anius."

"For what, my love?" he asked while he rubbed her stomach gently.

"For loving me, for standing by me. I do not deserve you," she said tenderly.

"We deserve each other and happiness for as long as we can have it. I love you always, Danara. You are and will forever be the queen of my heart." He kissed her head.

"I love you too, Anius, eternally. Please never forget that," she said before falling asleep peacefully in his arms.

The following day, everyone was overjoyed to see the king and queen happily together like they used to be. The only person that was unhappy was Alexander. He watched them from the castle entrance. They were in the stables. Danara tended to the horses with Anius at her side. She looked happier than she'd been in months. This vexed Xander. He could clearly tell that something had changed between them, overnight.

"I don't know what you said to her but I am so relieved to see Anius alive and well," Josephine hugged Xander surprising him.

"I cannot take credit. There certainly is a higher power at work. You know Danara yields to no one yet look at her now, the happy, dutiful wife," Xander said annoyed.

"Be careful, brother. You sound bitter about Anius' very fortunate events. I caution you not to wear your heart on your sleeve," Josephine answered waving at Anius who had just spotted them.

"I find it very sad that all you do is mind other people's business. Must be very lonely being you," Xander said coldly as he watched Anius and Danara mount a horse together. Anius lovingly kissed his wife's hands after she wrapped her arms around him to hold on.

"What I find pathetic is the fact that you are still here when you are not needed or wanted. You have no purpose here. You-are-useless! You already failed her, so do us all a favor and leave!" Josephine shouted causing Anius and his guards to come over.

"What did Alexander do now?" Anius asked riding toward them.

"He still breathes!" Josephine said, then pushed Xander out of her way and walked inside of the castle.

"Karo, stay close to her," Danara ordered. Karo obeyed and went inside after Josephine.

"Don't worry about her, she will be fine. Shouldn't Karo stay with you?" Xander asked unbothered by his sister's outburst.

"We wish to spend some time alone. Karo and the guards will remain here," Anius answered.

"Is that wise?" Xander tried to sound concerned when he really was jealous. He wanted to be the one spending time alone with her.

"I am more than capable of keeping the king safe," Danara joked. Aries erupted into laughter as he and the guards joined them.

He ordered the guards to take a post outside the castle since they were not needed at the moment.

"She's certainly right about that. Go on, you two. I will keep this one out of trouble," Aries said slapping a heavy hand on Xander's shoulder.

"Thank you, Aries. Apparently, someone needs to," Anius said then rode off with his love. Xander pushed Aries' arm off of him.

"You are going to have to do something about that," Aries said.

"Do something about what?" Xander answered irritated.

"Your anger since you clearly haven't been able to fuck it out of your system with nearly every woman in the kingdom. Let us try my way, I'll get you right."

"Why does everyone assume to know what I need? I am not angry. I am tired. Tired of my family and tired of this kingdom!" Xander shouted.

"First off, I never presume to know what others think. All I know is war and you are a soldier without one. I can tell by your actions that you may benefit from trying my way to get whatever you are experiencing out of your system," Aries answered.

"I'm almost afraid to ask, but what exactly is your way?" Xander asked feeling relieved to not be judged by him.

"First, we drink, then we find someone to pound on," Aries said leading the way.

"If this is your way of keeping me out of trouble, I approve," Xander happily followed.

"I hoped you might. I told you war, anger, and killing—those are my specialties." Aries laughed, then told the guards that they would return shortly. He and Xander mounted their horses and rode off.

Josephine walked alone in the forest near the castle. She was so angry with Xander. She tried to take her frustration out on the trees in the forest with her power but she could not focus.

"You shouldn't be out here alone." Karo startled her.

"Dammit, Karo, you scared me. What are you doing here?" She clutched her chest.

"I apologize for scaring you. The queen ordered me to stay close to you. What are you doing out here?"

"I can look after myself."

"I am well aware of your capabilities. However, I must obey my queen," he answered. For once, she didn't know how to respond. Her family didn't view her as capable to do anything on her own, not even with her newfound power.

"So, are you going to keep me in suspense?" he said lightening her mood.

"I needed a safe space to practice. I'm trying to use my power but I struggle controlling it when I'm upset."

"How did you control it before?" he asked.

"You know what, Karo, you wouldn't believe me nor understand." She sat down in the grass.

"Try me. After all that I've seen and experienced, do you really think I wouldn't understand?" Karo said thinking of when Danara resurrected him.

"You are correct. If anyone can relate, it would be you. I did not suddenly acquire this power as my brother did. I had to go through these trials. Every power that I acquired, I died for, then was resurrected and had to keep dying until I could control it. I can't even tell you how many times I died, I lost count, but I suffered every time." Karo put his arm around her neck and she rested her head on his shoulder.

"That sounds absolutely horrible. I know why you did it but still, I can't imagine how hard that was for you." He genuinely felt for her.

"It was horrendous," she whispered.

"So, you were able to control it under distress?" he asked.

"Yes, but it took time and I was so angry. The Lord literally intervened or else, I would probably still be in the trials." She shuddered thinking of the fire burning her flesh and the wind peeling off her skin.

"Well, you're angry with Xander now. Use that," Karo said standing, then helped her up.

"I want you to focus as hard as you can on hitting that tree." He pointed at the tree in front of them.

"This is ridiculous. I cannot do this right now," she said already discouraged.

"If you cannot control your abilities because of your emotions, then how will you defend your family when the time comes? Get out of that negative mindset and focus."

Josephine knew that he was right. She calmed herself and tried.

"Focus all of your energy on this oak tree. Think of nothing else," he said, then she tried her best to focus but still struggled. Karo put his hand on her stomach.

"This is where your energy comes from. Will it from here and it shall be done," he said confidently. She closed her eyes and did exactly what he said. The tree began to shake.

"It's working!" She beamed with excitement. "I . . . I don't know what to will it to do. I thought I could only control elements." She pointed both of her hands at the oak tree.

"Sounds like you set boundaries on yourself that God did not. Trust your instinct," Karo said firmly. She raised the large tree from the ground. It was so big it cast a shadow over them.

"Extraordinary!" he said, excited to see her power.

"Now that's odd. Look at the purple color at the roots," Josephine said placing the tree down in another spot. They both went to where the tree once was. The ground was surrounded by purple flowers. "These are verbena, also known as holy herb or devil's bane. They are very rare," she said inspecting it.

"I've never heard of it. What is its purpose?" Karo asked.

"It can be used to conduct or direct magical energy. Danara's aunts are always surrounded by it. Some believe it was used to staunch Jesus' wounds after he was removed from the cross. We did not find this by accident," she said as Karo took the herb from her hand and inspected it also. His fingers immediately felt a stinging sensation causing him to drop the plant.

"What happened?" Josephine quickly checked on his hand.

"I am fine, it was just a sting. That herb definitely has some kick to it." He chuckled.

"We should take some back with us." She said gathering as much as she could fit in her pockets. Karo suddenly began to shout. Josephine saw his fingertips that had touched the herb began to turn black. Karo began to heavily sweat.

"We have to get back to the castle now!" she said in fear for his life. Karo took her by the waist, then within seconds, they were home. He ran so fast she didn't realize what was happening until they were safely back. Karo fell to the ground shouting and holding onto his arm as the black stain on his fingertips began to cover his entire arm.

"Help us! Get the doctor," Josephine shouted at the guards as his health continued to deteriorate before her.

Anius and Danara rode to an old lake with a beautiful waterfall. It was far from the castle. As teenagers, they would come here for privacy.

"Oh my, we haven't been here in ages. It's so peaceful here," Danara said as he helped her off the horse.

"We could both use some peace," he said leading her to the lake. He took her shoes off and washed her feet in the water. She laid back staring at the sky.

"Thank you so much, that felt amazing," she said as he laid next to her.

"You don't have to thank me. I just want you to feel good," he said happily.

"I definitely do, thanks to you. I wish that every day could feel like this." She smiled.

"I will do my best to make that so, my love," he said rubbing her stomach.

"The child truly favors you. You are the one keeping me calm, controlling my urges," she said honestly.

"She will be as beautiful as her mother," he said.

"She? Anius, you must be mistaken. Luc . . . he said that I would give birth to a boy," she said confused.

"He does not know everything. Trust me, he is wrong. From the moment I placed my hand on your stomach before the phoenix restored you, I saw her. She will be magnificent and I will love her as my own. I already do and she feels that," Anius said kissing her belly causing it to feel warm and calm. Danara wanted to cry; his compassion was inspiring. She thought of how lucky she was to have such an amazing man. She stroked his hair, then he began to kiss her softly on her neck, her face, and her lips. Every kiss made her heart skip a beat. She felt a warm sensation between her legs, then got on top of Anius and ripped his shirt off. He stopped her.

"Please do not treat me like I'm broken," she said sadly, then got off of him.

"You are not broken. You are the strongest person I have ever known," he said assuredly.

"Then why did you stop me? Is it the child? Do you no longer desire me because of what he did to me?"

"It is not because of *our* child nor is it because I don't desire you. I always want you. What Lucifer did to you has made you doubt who you are and what you mean to me. I've waited all our lives to make love to you so understand that when that sacred moment happens, it will not be here outside in the grass nor in the heat of the moment. You are my queen, I can never treat you like anything less than that." His tone was so soothing she knew he spoke the truth.

"When I make love to you, wife, it will be exactly the way that you deserve." He kissed her tenderly.

"Honestly, something does not feel right. We should head back," he said now feeling alert like danger was close.

"I feel it too now," she said, then suddenly, her left arm began to throb and burn. "Karo is hurt. He's dying, I can feel him fading."

Aries and Xander entered the castle bloody and drunk singing songs of war. Aries quickly noticed the entrance was without guards.

"I see I have to whip these asses into shape," Aries barked.

"Where the hell are the guards?" Xander shouted, then laughed at his own echo. They heard a commotion coming from the main hall. When they stepped into the room, all of the guards were hovering over Josephine holding Karo down while he shouted in pain. Xander had to stop himself from vomiting when he saw Karo's arm.

"What the fuck is that?" Xander asked disgustedly.

"He's been poisoned by the verbena flower. I don't know how to help him." Josephine panicked.

Danara and Anius suddenly appeared.

"Karo!" Danara kneeled to aid him.

"Don't touch him!" Josephine shouted. "He touched the verbena flower and it did this to him. It keeps spreading. It started at his fingertips. I think it's reacting to his blood." Josephine was so afraid for his life. Danara saw that the poison now spread to his forearm and a long black vein appeared to be going toward his heart.

"We must stop this from spreading," Danara said nervously.

"What do I do? This is all my fault. He can't die because of me," Josephine pleaded.

"Karo, look at me," Danara said but he was unresponsive. "I am so sorry for this," she said, then quickly grabbed Aries' ax and chopped off Karo's arm.

It took two days of Danara feeding Karo her blood for his arm to begin to regenerate. She was exhausted. Anius tried to stop her nearly the entire time out of fear of losing her but she was defiant. She felt a deep bond with Karo. He was the only one she turned and could not let him die. She felt responsible for his life. Danara did not rest until he showed signs of his health progressing. Anius tucked her into bed and handed her a glass of water. Her throat was so dry it hurts to drink.

"I know what you need, my love," Anius said handing her a glass of what looked like red wine. Her senses awakened by the sweet aroma she instantly sat up licking her lips. She grabbed the glass of blood from Anius, then devoured it. Her body quivered in delight until she felt embarrassed for taking pleasure in something so grotesque in front of Anius.

"I'm sorry, I didn't realize how hungry I was." She shied away. Anius removed his white handkerchief, then gently wiped a drop of blood from the corner of her mouth. He looked at her so lovingly.

"You do not have to apologize for anything. I understand that this is what you need to sustain life so I give it to you with no judgment." He kissed her softly. "Do you feel better?"

"Yes, much better. Where did you get the blood from?" she asked.

"Aries and Xander actually gave me the idea. They hunted down some fugitives the day Karo got hurt. They were set to be executed today. The prisoners were murderers that eluded capture. I had one drained but not completely. I know that you may require his soul for your hunger to be completely satisfied. He's in prison when you are ready."

Danara kissed him. "You are amazing. Thank you so much. I wish I would have thought of that before I killed so many."

"Stop it," he said immediately. He would not allow her to punish herself anymore.

"You could not control your rage or hunger before. You are in control now and we can only move forward. God has provided a way," he said with such sincerity and conviction that Danara began to remember what it was like to have faith again.

Josephine awoke well-rested in her own bed. She was unsure of how she got there. The last thing she remembered was caring for Karo. She slowly sat up, then noticed Karo sitting in a chair across from her.

"You are stunning even when you sleep," he said coming closer. "May I sit?" he asked politely. Josephine nodded in agreement.

"You were really adorable also while you snored." He chuckled, then she playfully struck him with her pillow.

"I see you have your sense of humor as well as your arm back, smart ass." She smiled.

"Yes, but seriously, I wanted to thank you for taking care of me. When I awoke, you were asleep at my bedside so I carried you here. I hope that's alright. I thought I'd return the favor and make sure you were cared for as well. If there is anything that you need, I will make sure that you have it," he said so sweetly she couldn't stop herself from blushing.

"You are a true gentleman. Thank you. I'm glad you've recovered. I feel responsible for what happened. It was careless of me to allow you to touch the verbena flower," she said with much regret.

"Please, do not blame yourself. You would not have let me touch it had you known what it would do to me. I am healed thanks to you and Danara so do not dwell on this. I know you, woman, let the guilt go." He smiled showing his adorable dimples.

"I appreciate you acknowledging that. I would never let any harm come to you. I never witnessed how powerful the verbena was. I fear for what I will have to use it for." Karo could sense her sadness.

"I promise you, Josephine, whatever it is, you will not have to face it alone," he said making her smile.

"May I kiss you?" he asked sweetly.

"Yes." She leaned forward. "I love that you are so sweet and polite but you never have to ask me again," she said, then Karo kissed her so passionately she thought this was by far the best kiss of her life.

Danara slept most of the day undisturbed, then awoke late that night after midnight vomiting profusely. Josephine made her an herbal mint tea that helped with nausea.

"I'm sorry you are so sick, sister. This is perfectly normal with pregnancy. I promise this will soon pass," Josephine said as she helped Danara change from her sweat-soaked nightgown into a fresh one.

"You are a godsend, Josephine. Thank you. I'm sorry Anius woke you, he was so worried," she said weakly.

"Nonsense, this is why I'm here. I do not mind taking care of you. Try to rest. I've told your maidens to keep the tea warm in case you're in need of more. Sleep well," Josephine said, then hugged her and left the room. She told her brother he could enter.

"Finally, the vomiting has stopped. How are you, my love?" He laid down beside her.

"Better, but still terrible. I just want this to be over," she answered almost in tears.

"I'm sorry, my love, God willing it won't be much longer," he said kissing her forehead.

She tried to go back to sleep but her stomach kept cramping so Anius ordered her maidens to prepare a hot bath in the caldarium. The caldarium bathroom was very large and retained heat. Anius took long hot baths there after training or battle. The heat always helped with his muscle ache so he thought it would help with her pain.

"Rest easy, sweet child. Your mother is exhausted," Anius said rubbing her stomach gently and kissing it. He had such a way with the child. Danara felt that he really loved it and she knew the feeling was mutual. The child was moving around more than normal which caused her great pain. Her maidens let them know the bath was ready.

"Alright, my love, let's go." Anius carefully picked her up and carried her out into the hallway where four royal guards were waiting.

"I can carry her for you, sire," one of the guards offered.

"Never touch my wife," Anius said, then walked past him.

"You are incorrigible." Danara giggled.

"I meant it, woman." They laughed as they walked through the corridor. Three of her maidens and the royal guards followed closely. Anius pulled her body closer, then squeezed her gently.

"You are so light I can throw you in the air and catch you with one arm." He smirked.

"Anius, don't!" she said with panic in her voice. He laughed at her.

"I'm not going to do it but you know I could. I wield axes heavier than you," he boasted. Danara playfully hit him.

"Seriously, my love, you know I'd always catch you. I love you infinitely. When my heart ceases to beat, I will love you still. Whatever happens in our next life, I will find you. Say you know this to be true," he said confidently. Danara did not say a word. She thought of how her soul was damned. Hell was where she was heading if her life ever ended. This thought saddened her. Anius stopped walking. Their guards and maidens stopped as well.

"I know that I'm not going to live forever," he began.

"Anius, I do not want to talk about this." The thought of losing him caused her heart to ache. She would rather die than live any life without him.

"If you cannot speak on this, then there is still fear in you, so it's a conversation that we will absolutely have. God made you fearless, Danara. Having you in my arms right now is a miracle so I believe anything is possible. There is an afterlife and it is eternal. I will spend that eternal life finding you, then loving you. Our love defied the devil himself so when I tell you that whatever happens next I will find you, I want you to believe that undoubtedly. You of all people should not have any doubts. God plucked you out of hell twice. He has shown you who you belong to. Say you believe me or we are not moving." Anius meant every word and would not move. He waited for her to remember her journey. This was important to him because as husband and wife, they were made for each other and are now one. When one felt weak, it was the other's job to build them up—that was the vow they made before God so Anius was doing as promised, lifting her up because she needed him too even if she didn't know it. She did not feel certain but she listened to him and thought about all they'd been through and that he loved her still and he loved her child. God did rescue her from Lucifer, then delivered her from the evil that gripped her and made her lose her way. She had not realized until now that she was blessed and highly favored. This made her believe again.

"I believe you, Anius," she said without any doubt.

Anius leaned in and kissed her tenderly. His tongue gently caressed hers, then he placed his lips on hers and exhaled into her mouth causing a warm sensation that went through her body until it reached her heart and his love was received. Her shattered heart was whole again. He left her speechless, then began to walk again. The guards followed. Danara's maidens looked at each other wide-eyed, blushing and whispering about the passionate kiss they had just witnessed. One of the guards noticed the maidens were not following. He gave them a disapproving glance causing them to start walking and catching up. Anius carefully carried his love into the beautiful gold-decorated caldarium. He brought her to a square-shaped bath surrounded by large white pillars, then gently placed her on the edge of the hot tub. At first, he only put her feet in the water so her body would get used to the temperature.

"Thank you, love, you have been so attentive. Try to get some rest, I won't be long," she said, then felt a slight pain and clutched her stomach.

"Give us some privacy," he ordered the guards. They obeyed and posted outside of the room.

"You can leave us as well," he excused the maidens, then sat beside his wife.

"I'm not going anywhere, my love. I will bathe you myself and rub all of your aches and pains away." He kissed her cheek, then removed his shirt exposing his chiseled muscular body. Danara stared delightedly.

"I cannot focus when you look at me that way," he blushed.

"Well, I can't help the way I look at you, you're beautiful." She smiled.

"That's it, you're making this very difficult, get in the water, tease," he said, then got into the tub and carefully helped her in.

"Anius, we still have our clothes on," she giggled.

"That's exactly the point. Now stop distracting me and let me take care of you," he said, then grabbed the soap and massaged it into her hair gently caressing her scalp. She was completely relaxed and no longer felt pain. He proceeded to massage her neck, then held her from behind rubbing her stomach.

"How is that?" he whispered.

"Incredible," she answered, then turned around to face him.

"Are you going to take my dress off now, or should I?" She wrapped her arms around his neck.

"I would love to but for now, I have to make sure you are well," he said wanting to express his love for her yet still held back. His concern for her well-being was greater than his need to fulfill his desires.

"I promise you I feel so much better. I don't want you to be afraid to touch me or make love to me. I want you too."

"I am not afraid, my love. Just cautious. As much as I desire you, I can wait as long as it takes until I know for sure that you are ready. Meaning, your body not in pain, your mind no longer doubtful, and your heart open to receive my love and reciprocate," he answered sweetly.

"Hmm, I know what the problem is now. Stop talking and listen," she said, then took off her dress and placed her husband's head over her heart. He held her body close to his and pressed his ear on her chest. The sound of her heartbeat echoed in his ears sending vibrations to his awaiting heart. There were no more words between them. He listened to exactly what her heart told him to do. She was ready and he knew just how to touch her, how to kiss her, and how to love her. She reciprocated knowing exactly how to express all of her love to the love of her life.

The following day seemed like a dream. They spent the morning making love and slept all afternoon. By the evening, they were too tired to leave their bed so they dined there together. The guards were ordered not to allow any interruptions. Anius wanted his wife all to himself and she wanted the same. No one was permitted to disturb them. Only the maidens were allowed inside to change their sheets as they both took a soothing milk bath, then waited on the balcony while the maidens tidied up.

"Is this real?" Danara asked feeling so joyful she hoped it wasn't a dream.

"This is absolutely real, my love," Anius said kissing her head as he held her in his arms and they gazed at the starry night sky. "I honestly did not think I could love you more, wife, but I feel so deeply connected to you now. I cannot wait until they're done cleaning the room so I can get you back into the bed if that's alright with you."

"You can have me now, husband." She turned and kissed him softly on his lips. He removed her white silk robe and placed it on the edge of the balcony. The wind quickly took hold of it. Anius tried to grab it but the wind blew it down beneath them.

"You are definitely getting me another one." She laughed as they watched it blow away toward the garden.

"Is there someone out there?" Danara asked. She thought she saw shadows moving.

"I think so. Who's out there?" Anius shouted. "Looks like someone was fooling around in the bushes. It must be Xander," he said as two figures moved closer. The woman picked up Danara's robe, then walked into the moonlight.

"So, I guess this means you two are still alive," Josephine teased holding Danara's robe. Danara turned red blushing.

"I had no idea my brother was such an animal. Were you just going to take her right there on the balcony? That is no way to treat a queen," Josephine said, then they all burst into laughter.

"You are the queen of deflecting. Who were you kissing in the bushes? Mother would not approve of this behavior," he joked. Danara pinched him. Josephine covered her face embarrassed. She had hoped not to be seen by anyone. She had no idea if her siblings would approve. Karo slowly stepped out of the bushes.

"Your highness, forgive me, I can explain," Karo said with his head down. Danara could not stop laughing.

"I would love to hear this explanation. So, your tongue accidentally fell into the mouth of the king's sister?" Danara teased.

"Is that what we are to understand?" Anius chimed in.

"Please do not encourage them," Josephine said to Karo making Danara laugh harder.

"Go back to your room, both of you," Josephine said, then controlled the wind causing it to carry Danara's robe back to her.

"Showoff!" Anius shouted at his embarrassed sister.

"Don't be jealous, brother. It does not suit you," she said waving goodbye. "Danara, we will talk tomorrow, I'm going to ignore my fool of a brother and go to bed. Goodnight all," Josephine said walking away.

"You'd better be going to bed alone," Anius yelled so his sister could hear him. "By the way Karo, if whatever you have going on with my sister ends badly, I will have you hung," Anius said seriously.

"Is he kidding?" Karo asked Josephine following her inside.

"Oh, he's very serious but don't worry, you're immortal," Danara shouted giggling.

"Then I'll hang your immortal ass twice," Anius reiterated.

"You are both horrible. Go to sleep, losers," Josephine shouted as they entered the castle.

"Now that was fun." Danara smiled as her husband pulled her close.

"It certainly was. How long do you think that's been going on?" he asked removing her dark flowing hair from her eyes.

"I have no idea but I'll be sure to get all the details tomorrow as will she about you," she said peeking into their room. The maidens were done and had left the room.

"That's troubling. Say good things about me, wife."

"I'll think about it," Danara joked.

"Now I feel like I have something to prove, woman."

"Come prove it," she said, then walked into their bedroom and removed her gown letting it drop to the floor. Anius quickly followed his wife inside, then undressed and tenderly made love to her until the sun came up.

For the next five days, everything was peaceful. Danara felt like a brand-new woman and Anius was beyond happy as well. Life was good until the sixth day.

Danara awoke around midnight to the worst stomach cramps. Anius was awakened when he heard her painful moans.

"I'm going to get the physician," he said concerned.

"No, it will pass. Please stay with me." She laid her head on his chest.

"Whatever you want, my love. I will stay with you but if that pain gets any worse, I'll have to get him. I don't want anything to happen to you."

"I just want to lay in your arms. You are all I need." She kissed his bare chest and laid her head back down on it.

"I feel the same way," he answered. Danara slowly sat up when she realized he had no heartbeat.

"It's good to know you've enjoyed our time together. However, I do not think your husband would approve, my beauty." He smiled.

Danara froze. She wanted to scream. This was not her Anius; it was Lucifer. She tried to get up but he pinned her down to the bed.

"Not only did I take your virginity but now I've also been the first man you have made love, too. Anius will be so disappointed." Lucifer laughed in her face.

"Liar!" she whispered, barely able to get a sound out.

"You know I am telling the truth. I am the one you made love to in the caldarium and in your bed. You knew it was me the entire time just as you knew it was me now."

"You're a liar!" she screamed.

"You enjoyed it," he said muffling her mouth. "You and our child belong to me," he said, then roughly placed his hand on her stomach. The baby began to move erratically. Danara was terrified as she watched her stomach grow right before her eyes, then she passed out.

Danara awoke to the worst stomach cramps around midnight. Anius quickly awoke when he heard her painful moans.

"I'm going to get the physician," he said concerned. Danara remained silent. She looked at him with fear written all over her face.

"What is it? Is it the baby?" he asked frantically. She would not allow him to touch her.

"You are not Anius . . . You're not my husband!" she yelled at him. "Karo!" she screamed. Karo barged into the room within seconds quickly running to her side.

"What is it, my queen?" Karo asked as guards rushed into the room with Josephine.

"That is not Anius," Danara said to Karo. He immediately stood in front of her to defend her and the child.

"Let us all keep our cool. Guards, give us a moment," Josephine said, then the guards left waiting outside the room.

"Karo, I want to leave," Danara shouted.

"No! *Wait!* Danara, it's me," Anius begged her to believe him.

"No, you're not. You are Lucifer. This just happened . . ." she said putting her hand on her head confused. "This part didn't happen but we were laying there in the bed and you were not you," she screamed.

"Your highness, please calm yourself. I can sense that you and the child are in distress," Karo said worriedly.

"Danara, I swear to you, it's me. I think you had a nightmare. How can I prove to you that I am your husband?" Anius begged but she would not listen. She knew it was not a nightmare. Lucifer was there in her and Anius' bed. She could still feel his hands on her body.

"My king, please do not come closer. I must defend her from all that means harm. That includes you, sire," Karo said prepared to attack anything and anyone that approached his creator, his queen.

"Dammit, Karo, listen to me. She doesn't know what she's saying. I am not Lucifer," Anius said now agitated.

"With all due respect, King, she thinks that you are the demon. I am compelled to obey her every command and right now, she sees you as a threat. I will take her someplace that she feels safe," Karo said respectfully.

"Danara, I promise you, that is my brother. Please tell me what happened." Josephine moved closer.

"Josephine, don't!" Karo said firmly. He felt his body ready to leap at either one of them that dared to approach. He tried with everything in him not to hurt them but his need to defend Danara was *absolute*. He would kill them both if he had too.

"*Karo*!" Danara said in a weak voice. She almost fell over, but Karo caught her in time. Her stomach ached terribly. He . . . did something to me." She cried as Karo held her.

"Danara, I would never hurt you. You know that," Anius said sincerely.

"Karo, you cannot take her. Can't you see that she is not well?" Josephine said afraid for Danara and the child. Karo tried to ignore her words but he knew that she was right. He could feel Danara getting sicker every second. She was now too weak to stand. The room began to spin. She wanted to order Karo to get her out of there but the pain was too strong. Her body gave out and she passed out from the pain.

She awoke moments later. Once she came to, Josephine, Karo, and Anius were at her bedside. She noticed that she was not in her and Anius' bedroom.

"Do not move," Josephine said immediately. "I need you to listen to me carefully," she said slowly. "We had to remove you from the castle for your own safety and the sake of everyone else. We're in the tower right now."

"I do not understand," Danara said trying to sit up but she felt so much pressure in her stomach that she could barely move.

"Please, Danara, it is imperative that you remain calm," Josephine insisted. Danara became agitated.

"Get your hands off of me," she yelled at Josephine.

"Karo, help me up," Danara commanded. Karo cautiously helped her sit up. That's when she noticed that her stomach had greatly expanded. It was so big she looked like she was ready to give birth.

"Lucifer did this!" Danara panicked. Josephine and the others looked at each other but no one spoke. They all then stared down at her causing Danara to look down and further inspect. She noticed that to the left and right side of her bellybutton was two points sticking out. She ran her fingers over the points instantly knowing that they were horns.

"*Kill it! Get it out of me!*" she screamed hysterically. Josephine and Karo struggled to hold her down while Anius watched with no emotion on his face.

"You have to kill it!" she cried, trying to fight them off and attempted to kill the demon child herself but she was too weak. "Karo, kill it. I command you!" she shouted.

"My queen, I would do anything you command but I am forbidden from harming you or the child. I am compelled to disobey any such order," Karo answered putting his head down.

"You are useless! I should have let Lucifer take your soul," she yelled at him, then tried again to move but she couldn't. Everyone fell silent when they heard horrible sounds coming from her stomach. Danara froze. At first, she thought that she was hearing things so she stayed quiet and listened. Her stomach let out a loud growl that did not sound human. They were all frozen in fear. Danara suddenly clawed at her stomach digging her nails into her skin. She wanted to get the evil out of her by any means.

"Danara, please stop or we will have to restrain you," Josephine pleaded. Her heart broke for her but she was certain that no matter what happened, the unborn had to be protected.

"Anius, help us hold her down!" Josephine shouted at her brother. He remained in shock unable to speak or react. He was so overcome with guilt and grief. He felt that this was all his fault and thought he should never have let Phoenix restore her. This child was an abomination. He could no longer understand why God would allow it to live.

"*Anius!*" Josephine shouted. She gave up on reaching him and turned to Karo.

"Do it!" she demanded. Without question, Karo reached behind Danara's bed and grabbed two silver chains that were connected to the wall, then cuffed both of her hands so she could not hurt the child or herself. She tried to break free but the child was draining her energy and she was weak from not feeding so the shackles were able to hold her. Anius could not bear to see her chained or suffering. He walked out of the room without a word.

Once Xander got word of what happened, he rushed to the tower to see Danara. Josephine and Karo allowed him to be alone with her while she was sedated. He tried his best to hold back his emotions when he saw her. He was filled with anger when he saw her chained to the wall like an animal. He called her name when he entered the room. She did not say anything. She just stared blankly at the ceiling, appearing as if there was no life left inside of her. He truly pitied her when he got closer and saw the horns of the demon's evil seed nearly poking out of her stomach.

"This is wrong," he said angrily, then sat on the bed beside her. "I am so sorry," he said sadly as she continued to stare distantly as if he wasn't there. Her stomach growled loud. The sound was so horrific Xander quickly got up.

"Did you hear that? I know you heard it," she said calmly, then looked toward him and chuckled. "They all know there is a monster growing inside of me yet they let it live and chained me to the wall like I am the monster. Why do they continue to punish me, Xander? How can they tell whose will they serve? Does this look like the will of God?" she asked as tears fell down her face. Xander could not find words to console her. This was inhumane. He knew that she did not deserve this.

"Why did you come here?" she asked trembling. He wiped her tears.

"I came to fulfill a promise," he answered honestly.

"You . . . you came to help me?"

"I gave you my word that I would."

"But you can't. No one can help me," she sobbed.

"I can. Tell me what to do. How do I kill it?" He was willing to do anything for her.

"There is no killing it. Even your brother and sister know that," she said feeling hopeless.

"Then drink. You are too weak and they know it. Drink from me. Make me stronger. I will protect you and find a way to destroy that . . . monster."

"I can't. You know this blood is poison. I was wrong for making you promise that. I thank you for your loyalty, Xander. Please go." She felt so weak she could barely hold her head up.

"I have never known you to give up. Nothing and no one defeats you." Xander tried to remove her shackles but could not. He grabbed his small blade from its holster, then cut the palm of his left hand.

"Xander, don't!" Danara pleaded. She did not want to hurt him. The blood was too unpredictable, she was unsure of what it would do to him. The scent and sight of his blood started to take over her. All she could think of was to drain him. Xander slowly raised his hand to her mouth. She sucked the warm sweet blood savoring every last drop. Once she felt her strength return, she freed her hands from the shackles while never taking her mouth off of his hand. Xander's energy was nearly depleted.

"I feel weak," he said as he felt life leaving him.

"I will make you strong," she said, then drained him and cut her wrist with her sharp teeth. His body fell on the bed as he died. Danara hastily poured her poisonous blood into his mouth. She watched his chest as it quickly moved up and down, then it stopped completely. Xander's body was stiff. His soul emerged, then entered her body. She stood up regenerated. Anius entered the room with a fresh cup of blood in his hand. He dropped the cup as soon as he saw his brother's body on the bed not moving.

"What did you do?" he screamed at her.

"He helped me, so I gave him what he desired!" she shouted back.

"You killed my brother!"

"Xander is the only one that remained loyal to me. I would never end him. I made him greater than you," she snarled.

"Rise, Alexander! Free me from those that conspired against me," Danara commanded. Xander's body stood up. He grew ten times bigger in muscle and in height. He was so monstrous he towered over his brother. He leaped toward Anius causing him to ignite himself with the blue flame. Josephine and Karo charged into the room.

"*Traitors*!" Xander growled.

Josephine was terrified by his appearance. He stood nearly twelve feet tall. His body was large, muscular, and covered with grey fur. His hands and feet grew long, black curved claws. His teeth were replaced with long white fangs that protruded through his mouth. Josephine saw blood still wet on Danara's mouth and automatically knew what took place. Xander swiftly moved to Karo and tore a hole in his throat with just a swipe of his new paw. He snatched a chunk of his flesh and ate it in front of Josephine. She watched Karo's body fall to the floor as he held onto his throat trying to put pressure on his wound. She moved to help him but Xander grabbed her by both arms clutching her tight.

"Did I break your heart, sister?" Xander asked wiping Karo's blood from his mouth, then spread it on her face. She saw pure evil in his eyes. She understood now that whoever came in contact with Lucifer's blood would have a part of him inside of them. These black eyes that stared back at her piercing through her soul could only belong to the demon that stole everything from Danara. These were the eyes of Lucifer.

"Did you hear what I said, dear sister?" Xander laughed as he continued to transform before her. His hands and torso grew exponentially bigger. He grabbed Josephine by her neck forcing her to face him. She thought he meant to rip her head off. He enjoyed the look of horror on her face staring from beneath him. She wanted desperately to fight but she was emotionally broken and could not muster up the strength. Xander let her go, then returned to Karo's body leaning over him. Anius seized the moment and jumped on Xander's back putting him in a hold not to hurt him but to subdue him. Xander easily tossed his body with such force Anius was knocked unconscious. Xander returned to Karo's body that was weakened by his loss of blood but still had life in it. He laid there paralyzed in a warm pool of his blood.

"Hey, Karo, I heard you gave my sister your heart. Is that true?" he asked putting his ear next to Karo's mouth taunting him as he coughed on his blood.

"Xander, don't let Lucifer win over you. Karo and Danara resisted him, you can, too. Please don't kill him," Josephine begged for her lover's life. Xander ignored her pleas.

"I'm going to take your silence as a yes. So, you are fucking my sister. I'm not only going to kill you for betraying your queen. I am also destroying you because I do not approve of this relationship," Xander said, then ripped out Karo's heart and held it in his sister's face while it dripped with his fresh blood.

"Now you truly have his heart. Here, take it. It's yours, a gift from me to you," he said in a calm and eerie tone. Josephine screamed as Xander tried to stuff Karo's heart in her mouth. "I offer you one last kindness before I end your life for being a traitor, but as usual, you're an ungrateful bitch! Oh well, you and your three-day lover can burn in hell together eternally," he said, then reached over and tore her heart out as well. He tossed her lifeless body aside.

"Two traitors down, one to go." Xander laughed maniacally after he squeezed the last bit of blood from Josephine's heart into his mouth. He picked up Anius' body from the ground bashing his head against the wall until he was responsive.

"You are the biggest traitor of them all. You promised to love and protect Danara, then you let Lucifer steal her from you and impregnate her. Your betrayal didn't stop there, you then forced her to carry the little demon against her will. You are no better than the monster that raped her," Xander howled in his face as he wrapped his big strong arms around Anius squeezing his arms at his side.

"Don't worry, brother, now she will be with a real man. I swear I'll take way better care of her than you did," he said placing his knee in the middle of Anius' back, then pulled at both of his arms trying to tear them apart from his body. Anius ignited the blue flame. He struggled to get out of Xander's grip; his strength was too much for him. Xander felt the flame burning his flesh and still tightened his grip. He could tell by the look on Danara's face that she would attest to him killing his brother but it was too late. She had given him the one thing he wanted more than her—power. With this great power came an uncontrollable rage. The darkness in him that had always been tucked away was now able to do whatever he willed with no guilt or consequence. He smiled at Danara as his skin and flesh continued to burn. He tore at her husband's arms ferociously until he saw Anius' blood squirt on her face. That's when he realized he had torn his brother apart. He ripped off Anius' head with ease, then joined her.

"My queen, I sense you disapprove of my last kill. No worries, I am still going to honor my word and rid you of Lucifer's spawn," he said kneeling down in front of her facing her stomach. He dug his long, sharp claws into the top of her stomach, then moved his hands in a circular motion. Danara screamed in agony, then her body fell backward onto the bed. She watched Xander rip the child from her body. The last thing she saw was black blood slowly dripping off of the child exposing its sharp horns, then all went dark.

Danara opened her eyes moments later. She was still in the tower chained to the wall. She felt completely disoriented. She hardly noticed Xander's presence when he entered the room.

"This is wrong." She heard his voice echo in her mind but she felt stuck and couldn't move or answer him. She stared helplessly at the ceiling.

"I am so sorry, Danara." His voice echoed again, then she realized he was on the bed beside her. She stared distantly unsure of what was real. Her stomach growled loudly. The sound was so horrific Xander quickly got up. Danara now understood that she had already experienced this moment and what would follow is Xander executing everyone if she gave him her blood. She knew now that Lucifer was at work. He had found a new way to torture her.

"Tell me what to do, how do I kill it?" Xander pleaded.

"I know you are here, Lucifer. Show yourself!" she shouted. Xander continued to speak as if he did not notice her outburst. Danara frantically looked around the room. She looked toward her silver wrist cuffs that started to get hot. She was not startled when she saw Lucifer's reflection staring back at her.

"Look at what your so-called family has done to you, my beauty," Lucifer said sympathetically.

"I can free you from this. All you have to do is ask." He smiled.

Her senses picked up an overwhelming enticing aroma. She looked up and Xander's bloody hand was near her face.

"Drink. Make me stronger and I will protect you," Xander said as his blood dripped. Her mouth watered.

"Yes. Turn him or you can come and reign with me. Our child will be born soon. I can free you if that is what you wish. Just say the words." Lucifer went on," If you resist, you will relive this moment and your darkest nightmares endlessly. No one can save you and I will never stop coming for you, my beauty."

Danara felt her mind snapping. Both scenarios were frightening.

"Drink," Xander repeated with his bloody hand nearly touching her mouth as the demon laughed.

"Please God, help me!" she cried out.

"*God*! Have you learned nothing? God has forsaken you," he yelled causing her belly to ache. There was suddenly a loud crashing sound at the door. Anius entered the room rushing past his sister, Karo, and the guards. Upon entering the room, he saw Xander leaning over Danara trying to force his bloody hand in her mouth. Anius recognized the frightful gaze on Danara's face and followed her eyes. He saw Lucifer's reflection on her wrist cuffs. He sprang into action setting off a powerful blast of heaven's flame. The eruption knocked everyone around him backward, then melted Danara's shackles and violently threw Xander against the wall. Anius joined Danara who was the only one untouched by the blast.

"My love, forgive me. I lacked the courage to free you sooner," Anius said disappointed in himself.

Danara was furious with him for allowing them to chain her up but she was relieved that he came back for her. His love for her truly was undeniable.

"He cannot save you from me!" Lucifer shouted from inside her head. She placed her hands on her ears and screamed.

"Do not give him power. We can defeat him. Trust in God. Please trust me, once again," Anius said with his hands over hers. Danara trusted in her husband and allowed him to help her. He carefully lifted her up in his strong, capable arms, then blasted a hole through the wall with heaven's flame.

"Anius, don't do this! You cannot keep her safe alone," Josephine tried to reason with him.

"I am not alone. God is always with me. Do not follow for your own sake," Anius said firmly. Before Josephine could say anything else, he and Danara were gone.

Anius moved with a speed that even Karo could not keep up with. Danara burned with fever so he brought her to the lake with the waterfall, their secret place. The cool waters calmed her fever and her spirit. He took her behind the waterfall into a hidden cave where they played in their youth. He sat her down, then dried her with heaven's flame.

"That is so much better," she said feeling relief.

"I never should have let them chain you up like that," he said ashamed.

"I was afraid. I questioned my own faith when I saw what our choices did to you. I didn't know how to help nor would I be the one to imprison you. All I knew to do was go to church and pray for you," he said looking away.

"Lucifer tormented me with hallucinations. He made me watch as Xander killed you all. I was too afraid and desperate to be freed . . . I gave Xander my blood and he changed. He was horrific. He killed Josephine and Karo . . . he killed you, he killed all of you, then ripped the child from my womb with his bare hands. Lucifer would've made me relive that moment until I gave in and let him take me back to hell. You rescued me. I don't know what I would have done if you hadn't. I couldn't bear to watch you die again. This torment will never end. He said he will never stop." She sobbed. He sat down next to her.

"Please don't cry. I promise I will find a way to stop this. I will keep you safe." He looked at her stomach. "I am sorry you had to witness that. I can understand you were desperate to be freed, we left you no choice. I do not believe that you would give Xander your blood if you knew he'd kill us all."

"*Don't*! You always try to make me sound better than I am. I've done terrible things. I murdered the innocent. I have now earned my torment." She felt disgusted with herself thinking of all the bad things she had done.

"You've made mistakes as we all often do. None of us are perfect or have had to face what you survived. I won't have you bash yourself. We must focus on the present. I can sense that the child will be born soon. That's why I had to get you away from everyone. This responsibility is mine alone. Whatever happens, we face it together. God is with us. He is all we need," he reassured her, then rubbed her stomach when he saw the child move and cause her discomfort.

Danara felt an enormous amount of pressure at the bottom of her stomach.

"It's happening! The baby is coming!" She panicked.

Her husband remained calm for her. He saw that the child's horns were no longer visible. She shouted as the pain intensified. Anius inspected her. A large amount of blood gushed out. He could not see the child's head. The cave began to shake. Loud rumblings came from behind the waterfall. Day turned into night. Anius could hear Lucifer's minions howling from a distance.

"They are coming for us," she whispered.

Anius tried to think fast. He knew that she was right and also knew that the child was stuck inside of her. She pushed with all of her strength but nothing happened. Her body was exhausted.

"Stop!" he insisted. "Save your energy," he said calmly. "I'm going to have to take her out. I need you to focus on me, my love. Can you do that?" he asked as the ground beneath them shook. He ignored it. "Focus, Danara. Do you hear the waterfall? The sound of the water always calmed you. Close your eyes and listen to only that."

He was her pillar of strength. She closed her eyes and tried. She was so afraid but his calmness and confidence eased her fear. Anius took his blade from its holster, then sliced her stomach open. He reached inside of her stomach and felt the baby's head. Danara screamed as the strong vibrations radiating from her body shook the entire cave. Her body began to heal itself. Her womb closed with one of his hands still inside. He repeated the same incision that he had just made. The ground beneath them began to crumble. He quickly grabbed onto the baby with both hands as they all fell into the water. When they impacted the water, the baby was in his arms but Danara was gone. He got out of the water and wrapped his shirt around the baby, then surrounded her with heaven's flame creating a protective ring around her with it. He moved to jump back into the water for his love when he was suddenly attacked by the minions.

Danara watched helplessly from beneath the water. The water filled her lungs as she watched Anius attack the minions ferociously with only his hands. One by one, the minions fell into the water turning it red from their blood. She could no longer see her husband. She struggled to reach the surface. Her wound had not healed. Water continued to fill her lungs. She felt her body dying and knew that at any moment, she would be reunited with Lucifer in hell. She closed her eyes, then felt a tug at her arms. When she opened her eyes, it was Anius that she saw. He placed his lips on hers breathing life into her, then helped her to the surface.

"You're not healing!" He was surprised to see blood still pouring out of her. He picked her up holding her firmly in his arms. Danara was frightened when she saw Lucifer's minions. Anius knew there was no way out of this. His wife was bleeding profusely. The child cried in the distance as hundreds of minions surrounded. Anius looked to the dark sky and cried out.

"Father in heaven, please hear me. I trust in you completely and have followed you blindly with only my faith to guide me. The bible says that faith can moves mountains. There are hundreds of mountains standing between us and our daughter. You promised that faith greater than a mustard seed can move mountains. My faith in you is so great it can fill the entire sky. I'm going to continue to trust in you until my dying breath. I know you are with us so I have no fear. I humble myself before you and surrender." He prayed wholeheartedly, then paused for a moment and looked at his wife with an expression on his face that she had never seen.

"Anius, what is it?" she asked with desperation in her voice. Tears flowed down his face. He smiled at her, then spoke.

"He answered me!"

"Who? Anius who answered you?" she asked frantically.

"*God*!" Her husband finally answered.

"What did he say?" She clutched his face.

Anius began to walk through the crowd of minions unafraid as he repeated the words of God.

"God said to me . . . *Do not fear, for I am with you. Do not be dismayed for I am your God. I will strengthen you and help you. I will uphold you with my righteous hand.*" As Anius repeated the powerful words of God, he walked through the crowd with his wife in his arms. The minions fell dead at his feet. God did not allow any of Lucifer's minions to touch them. When they finally reached the child who was still surrounded by heaven's flame, all of the minions were dead. He placed his wife down and tried to heal her with the flame but it did not work.

"Father, please, I cannot lose her again," Anius begged God.

Danara's health continued to fade as the child cried hysterically. Anius took the baby into his arms. The baby's appearance changed by the second from human to a demon. Anius could feel that this was causing it pain and that the flame was also affecting it, but he had to keep the child safe and contained until he could figure out what to do next.

"Do not cry little one. I have you now," he spoke softly to the baby. "You remember my voice, don't you? I could always calm you when you were in your mother's belly. Do you remember that?" he said as the child continued to scream. Danara closed her eyes. It was at this moment that Anius truly understood his purpose.

"Stay with me, my love," he said gently touching Danara's face. She opened her eyes once more.

"So, listen little one, I was absolutely depending on God to intervene for us once again. I'll be honest with you. I have no idea what is supposed to happen but I just thought of something. We are all born into this world with free will. I had to make a choice to be your father and I truly believe that I made the right choice. I also believe that you are supposed to make a choice. You must decide what kind of person you are going to be. No matter what you choose, do not feel wrong about your choice. You are powerful, intelligent, and beautiful. All of God's creations are perfectly made in his image and he does not make mistakes. Understand, sweet child, you were meant to be. I won't lie to you. Things will be difficult with your mother and others accepting you but you are strong enough to handle anything. If you want, I will be there every step of the way to love you and guide you through life. I implore you, whatever you are battling inside, choose love and you will never feel alone because I will always be there for you and most importantly, so will God. I will teach you how important and kind he is when the time is right, but right now, your mother needs you. I can sense how incredibly powerful you are. I know you can choose to save your mother. I am going to put the flame out now because I do not wish to harm you.

I am sorry if I did," Anius said sincerely, then did as he said and extinguished the blue flame.

"Anius . . . don't," Danara protested. She did not trust the child of Lucifer.

"Please, Danara, trust me. Allow her to choose," he answered as the child continued to scream, then slowly took the form of a human child. Her horns were no longer visible. Anius sensed someone approaching and Danara's health fading.

"I . . . I can see the flames," Danara whispered faintly. Within seconds, Josephine and Karo appeared. Xander followed on a horse.

"Dear God, is she alive?" Josephine said immediately running to aid Danara. She had not yet realized the child in Anius' arms.

"Why isn't she healing? What do we do?" Josephine asked frantically trying to help her.

"She could not deliver the baby. I had to cut her out myself. She hasn't been able to heal since," Anius answered as the baby cooed in his arms. Josephine looked up at her brother finally realizing the baby was there.

"She's beautiful. Is she alright?" Josephine asked surprised that the baby was now here and even more surprised that it appeared to be human. They were alerted when they heard Xander's horse approaching. The baby felt uneasy and started reacting to Xander's presence. Anius and Danara looked at each other, then at the child as if they read each other's minds.

"Are you paying attention?" she asked him. Anius knew immediately they were in imminent danger. He nodded in agreement.

"Please, give her to me," Danara asked as Xander rode over.

"You all are incredibly hard to track," Xander said getting off of his horse. He stopped abruptly when he saw the baby in his brother's arms. He instantly thought of destroying it. He was not swayed by its human form. It was still Lucifer's child. He believed with everything in him that it should not be permitted to live. Anius handed the baby to his love.

"Are you certain that is a good idea? She tried to rip the child from her belly not too long ago." Josephine whispered her concern to Anius.

"Let them be," he answered sternly watching Xander closely from the corner of his eye.

"It is a tradition in my family to bless a new addition with God's word. I lost my way but today, because of you and Anius, I've found my faith again and although I was lost, God's words never left me." Danara smiled and spoke softly to her daughter.

"You have my mother's smile . . . and those eyes are unforgettable," she said as she reached into the lake nearby, then filled her hand with water and poured it on her daughter's head. Her daughter grew restless as she spoke.

"I will praise thee for I am fearfully and wonderfully made. Marvelous are thy works, and that my soul knoweth right well . . . My mother would have me recite this verse daily when I struggled with who I was and how I came to be. I know your struggle is far more complex, but you have us. Anius gave you a strong name, Sophia Grace. Sophia means wisdom and Grace means God's favor. Sophia Grace, you are loved and important. I can see that your soul is still struggling. If this is the end for me, the last thing I will do is free you from Lucifer's grasp. Your soul belongs to God."

"Danara, let me take her," Josephine asked. Every instinct in her body was letting her know danger was close. The sky was still black. There were no minions around, yet she knew something was coming.

"We should get them back to the castle," Josephine said. Anius grabbed her arm abruptly.

"You should stand your ground," he demanded.

"Easy, brother, she's right. Let us get them out of this cold end-of-the-world gloom. It's creepy out here. Danara does not look well. Karo, take the queen. I'll get the child," Xander said walking toward Danara and her daughter. Anius swiftly disarmed his brother grabbing his sword igniting it with heaven's flame.

"What has come over you?" Josephine shouted.

"Take another step, Alexander, and it will be your last," Anius said with certainty. He then turned to Karo. "You've already moved against your queen when you shackled her. Betray her again and I will drive this sword through your heart. We will test the limits of your immortality and see where it fares against God's flame."

Anius stood before Danara and the baby with his back toward them. He faced Karo and his siblings ready to strike them down if God so willed it. He was now fulfilling the promise he made to God when the phoenix returned Danara from hell and restored her. Anius was no longer just believing, he was acting on faith following the difficult path that God knew he would follow because he knew the strength that he put in Anius when he created him. Everything else Anius needed came from pain, loss, tragedy, and love. He understood now that everything he and Danara endured was necessary because it made him a powerful warrior for God. He was now claiming his position as Sophia Grace's Protector.

Danara continued to recite verses from the bible. The powerful words flowed through her as her body trembled.

"Anius, my dear brother, calm yourself. You know that I do not mean them any harm but I cannot say the same for your wife. Do not let her deceive you. We are not your enemies." Josephine tried to get the situation under control.

"You are the one who is deceived. Our brother plots this minute to end the child's life. *Open your eyes*! Do what you were trained to do. Either way, this is where I stand. I am Sophia Graces' protector, you would have to kill me to get to her. I promise you I will not be moved unless God moves me!" Anius said firmly keeping his eyes on the three of them.

"What is he speaking of, Xander? Is this true? You want to kill the baby?" Josephine pushed him.

"That evil spawn is turning us against each other," Xander lied.

Danara continued as the siblings argued. She placed her hand over the water, then recited another verse.

"Behold, I give unto you power to tread on serpents and scorpions and over all the power of the enemy, and nothing by shall any means hurt you." Once the words left her lips, the water began to move back and forth. Sophia screamed hysterically. Her eyes went completely black. Danara arose with Sophia Grace still in her arms. She exhaled, then bit into the baby's neck until she had her fill with the infected blood. Her wound finally healed and her energy was restored. Her daughter's blood was more powerful than Lucifer's. Danara struggled to overcome the urge to drain her.

"She's killing her!" Josephine said, then she and Xander ran toward Danara and the child. Anius stood between them and would not let them pass. He threw his sword toward Karo striking him in the stomach, knocking him down immediately neutralizing his biggest threat. He grabbed both of his siblings by their throats, then threw them so far away they were no longer in his view. Anius willed the sword to return to his hand and it obeyed.

"You'd better go catch them while you still have time," Anius said, then Karo took off running with incredible speed and caught Josephine and Xander right before their bodies impacted the ground. Anius continued to stand guard. He never turned around to face his wife. He trusted her and she trusted him to protect them.

"Finish this!" he shouted at Danara as he saw Karo returning with the others. Danara made her body fall backward into the water while she held on tight to Sophia. The water had now become holy. Danara had blessed the water when she recited the undeniable word of God over it. The blessed water burned her daughter's newborn skin. Sophia wailed. The sounds that came out of her were not human. Her screams filled the night sky sounding like multiple demons screaming at once. The bone-chilling sound froze all who heard it.

Danara and the child's head emerged from the water. The baby's skin was now black and oily, her horns were sharp and made of pure gold. Her fangs and nails were made of the same. Sophia gripped Danara's arms with her claws, then struck her in both eyes with the powerful unforgiving horns. Danara blocked out her excruciating pain tightening her grip on Lucifer's child.

"*You cannot have her Lucifer*!" Danara's voice roared like thunder. She stuck the baby's entire body above the blessed water. Her daughter fought back with incredible strength but was not stronger than the faith Danara now possessed. When she pulled her daughter out of the water, she was no longer a baby. She had aged seven years.

"Sophia Grace, hear me. I am your mother. The devil has a hold on you but I will not let him claim you. Fight with me. I love you. I feared you when I carried you, afraid of what you would become. I know now what Anius your father who chose to love you has always known about you. You are God's perfect creation born in his image. There is no evil strong enough to destroy that. There is nothing that can come between the love we all feel for you. I'm sorry I did not know how to love you sooner but I do now and that is eternal," Danara said as she hugged her daughter close no matter how many times Sophia clawed at her and bit into her flesh. Anius finally turned around when he heard Sophia's voice call out to Danara. He felt her strong spirit fighting back. Josephine stepped forward and willed Danara and Sophia out of the water with her mind. Anius stopped her causing their bodies to be suspended in the air.

"Do not interfere!" he ordered Josephine to stand down.

"I'm trying to help them. I thought Danara was killing her before but now I see she's saving her. Allow me to help. This is what I was trained for," Josephine pleaded.

"Josephine, sister, this is what Danara was chosen for. Don't you understand what's happening? Danara believes in God again. She has faith. He will not let her down. Watch him do his work," Anius said confidently.

"Mother!" Sophia cried as the demon inside of her fought for control of her. "Please, help me!" Danara saw a glimpse of her daughter looking back at her petrified. In an instant, Sophia resembled the horrific demon again. "Save me, mother! Save me!" the demon teased, then continuously bashed its head into Danara's.

"Josephine, bring them down," Anius demanded. Josephine tried but the demon inside Sophia was now in full control. Danara tried to force her back into the water but Sophia overpowered her. They fell to the ground instead. Anius quickly made a circular wall with the blue flame that surrounded only Danara and Sophia barring anyone from getting to them.

"She needs my help. The child is too powerful," Karo said worried for Danara.

"This is Danara's fight and she will be victorious," Anius answered firmly as Sophia continued to torture her mother trying to make her loosen her grip on her neck.

"Sophia Grace, I will never give up on you. I know you hate me. I deserve that. All I've shown you from the moment I knew you existed is hate. It was hard for me to accept you. I promise you with every bit of me I love you. You are the best part of me. Please give me a chance to prove to you what love is. I feel your strong spirit. You want to be freed of Lucifer's grasp. God will free you through me. The demon that controls your body does not believe in the power of God but we know and trust in him. He will deliver you from the evil that possesses you." Sophia instantly stopped attacking her. Danara loosened her grip.

"You love me? Sophia asked innocently.

"Unequivocally," her mother answered honestly. Sophia cried tears of blood.

"I love you too, mother. I want to be with you but the demon won't let me. He's too strong." Sophia continued to cry.

"That is exactly what he wants you to believe. We will be triumphant if we fight him together. You just have to believe." Danara held her daughter's face in her hands. She resembled Lucifer's horrible face but she loved her anyway. Danara kissed her forehead. Sophia's body flew backward out of Anius' protective flame causing it to extinguish. The bond between mother and child was so strong it scared the evil in Sophia. It wanted desperately to get away from Danara. Josephine blocked Sophia's path as Karo, Xander, and Anius surrounded her. Anius could not look Sophia in the eye. She resembled Lucifer so much this saddened him. He imagined how hard that must've been for his wife. He was proud of her. Instead of hate and disgust, she showed her daughter love and acceptance and was fighting with everything to save her.

"Do you really think you can stop me, witch?" Sophia paced back and forth taunting Josephine.

"Sophia, we do not want to hurt you," Josephine said calmly.

"Silence, witch!" Sophia said causing Josephine to choke.

Xander made eye contact with his brother. He looked down at his sword in Anius' hand, then again at his brother. Anius knew exactly what he was thinking.

"There is something I like about you, witch, so because of that, I will save you for last." Sophia's young menacing voice was haunting. "For now, I will kill the weakling first," she said setting her sights on Xander. Anius ignited the sword with his flame, then willed the sword into Xander's hand right before Sophia charged at him. She viciously slashed away at him with her pointy gold claws. Xander defended each blow as best he could but she was extremely fast. Karo grabbed her from behind after she slashed Xander across his chest. The scent of his blood drove Sophia crazy. Anius checked on his brother's wound as Karo held on tight to her.

"You can't hold me!" she shouted at Karo as he maintained his grip.

"You forget whose blood you get your strength from," Sophia said, then easily maneuvered out of his grasp.

"Kneel!" she commanded. Karo's body obeyed against his will.

"Sophia, don't," Josephine begged her.

"You love him, don't you?" Sophia asked. Josephine knew not to answer. Sophia whispered something into Karo's ear that no one else could hear. Karo suddenly leaped forward charging toward Josephine. Anius moved quickly to intercept but Karo moved like a man possessed. He took Josephine's head and slammed it onto the ground, then punched her in the stomach so hard her feet left the ground. Her entire body was thrown violently in the air. Anius leaped into action and stepped on Karo's shoulder with force giving himself a boost. He caught his sister mid-air, then landed on his feet.

"Enough!" Anius roared shooting his powerful flame at Karo incapacitating him. He then stood in front of Sophia prepared to die for his loved ones.

"Direct all of your anger toward me, coward. You know I can take it," Anius shouted at her.

"Look who finally has the courage to face me." She laughed.

"We both know I always had the courage, demon. You are the one who lacks courage, Lucifer. You are the coward hiding inside of an innocent child. How does it feel to finally have the weapon you have sought for centuries yet you lack the fortitude to wield it? Deep down inside of Sophia, there is still love and that is something you cannot abolish nor control. Release her. You have already lost this battle, accept it," Anius proclaimed. Sophia thrust her left arm into Anius' chest gripping his heart.

"I never lose!" Sophia shouted into his face with her father Lucifer's voice.

"*No!*" Danara shouted. Sophia threw his limp body onto the ground.

"Kill me! I am the only one that stands between you and fully controlling Sophia. If you want to walk this Earth, you will have to go through me," Danara challenged Lucifer. Sophia laughed.

"That's comical. You are no match for me. Just as you witnessed with Karo, I can control you. Without me, you have no power. In fact, I strip you of it." Sophia slowly walked toward her. Danara began to gag. All of Lucifer's blood that was inside of her spilled out onto the ground from her eyes, nose, and mouth. Sophia completely drained her. Danara's skin was dry and as wrinkled as a prune. She looked as though she had aged a hundred years. Sophia kneeled over her body.

"Now, you are powerless. Your love cannot save Sophia, she is mine. You cannot stop me, human. You have lost." She smiled proudly.

"You have forgotten that it is God who strengthens me and it's on his authority that Sophia is free to decide her own destiny. She has chosen love. She chose us. What God has brought together, let no man separate." A powerful beam of light shot from the sky turning darkness into light. The beam ignited Danara's body restoring her, then blessing her with a power greater than Lucifer's. She willed Sophia's body into her arms and held on.

"Release her!" Danara commanded electrifying her daughter's body as Lucifer refused to relinquish his hold. He felt Sophia fight back and was overpowered forcing him to flee from her body.

"Mother, we did it! I am free." Sophia said excitedly. She wanted to run into her mother's arms but Danara held her hand up stopping her.

"Stay back. Do not touch me," Danara shouted. "Anius, keep her safe," she said sadly.

"Lucifer is gone. Where are you going?" he answered already knowing her intention.

"He is not gone. He is in me. I can hear him in my head. She will never be safe around me. I trust you Anius, my love. I know you will do what is right." She slowly moved backward.

"You don't have to do this. I can help you," Josephine said approaching her dear friend.

"You cannot. He is too unpredictable. This is what you were both chosen for. I must stay away from everyone. I will not hurt you or any of you again," Danara said tearfully. Josephine put her arms around her holding her close.

"We are in this together. Trust us to help you, sister," Josephine concluded, then reached into her pocket for a concoction she made previously with the verbena flower. She rubbed it on her hands, then placed them over Danara's eyes uttering one word that made her collapse into Josephine's arms. The word that she said was *sleep*.

Danara awoke sometime later in a room unfamiliar to her. She was surrounded by servants. She noticed one of her servants abruptly leave to tell the others that she was conscious. She sat up feeling dizzy as her mind raced.

"My queen, I think you should remain in bed until the others arrive," her servant suggested cautiously.

"Where is my husband?" Danara insisted.

"I assure you, he will be here shortly," she answered nervously. Danara ignored her suggestion and still got out of bed, then left the room. She told the guards that were posted at her door not to follow her but they did anyway from a distance. She realized she was in the west wing of her castle near the guest quarters unable to comprehend why. She walked down the corridor until she came upon a staircase that led her down. She felt out of place and uneasy as she made her way down the stairs, then to the other side of the castle. She thought it odd that no one was around when she reached her and Anius' bedroom. She stopped immediately when she heard a peculiar sound.

"Your highness, the king has ordered all to stay away from this area," one of her guards cautioned.

"Why did he issue that order?" she asked but he put his head down not answering. Again, she heard the sound of someone wailing. She continued down the corridor, ignoring the guards advising against it. She proceeded down the servants' back staircase following the sound. Her guards ran after her when she reached the basement.

"Back off!" she ordered as her eyes shined a bright emerald green compelling them to obey unable to resist.

She continued down the long hallway passing empty prison cells that had not been used since her father was king. She now heard the sound of shackles moving, remembering when she was shackled in the tower before her daughter's birth. She came upon a large prison door and opened it with ease. There she saw Alexander having sex with one of her maidens. He growled like an animal as he thrust himself roughly inside of the maiden from behind pulling her hair as she moaned. Xander's appearance began to change drastically. He suddenly stood ten feet taller with his entire body now fully covered with grey hair resembling a giant wolf. He looked at Danara, then howled as he climaxed. Danara stepped into the room. The maiden saw her in the doorway and hurried to get dressed, then joined her queen.

"Are you alright?" Danara asked her concerned.

"My queen, you are awake!" she answered, then Xander growled at them. The maiden finally realized that he no longer appeared human yet she was unfazed.

"Did he hurt you?" Danara asked.

"I am so embarrassed that you saw me in such a state but you misunderstand. It was my choice and honor to lay with Alexander. I have never felt such pleasure," she answered happily, then left the prison cell grinning. Danara approached Alexander. He angrily slammed down the pure silver chains that bound him.

"Calm yourself, Alexander," she said as he pounded the wall with his large hairy fist. Anius and the guards filled the room agitating him more with their presence. He tried to rip his chains from the wall.

"Danara, you are not safe around him. He cannot control himself in this form." She heard Anius shout from behind her but she remained focused on Xander.

"Do not worry my love. He will not harm me," she answered with confidence. Xander became enraged as more soldiers entered the room.

"Stay back!" she ordered never taking her eyes off of Xander. His anger made him continue to transform. His head now reached the ceiling. Danara was the only one unafraid.

"I understand your struggle. The evil in your blood is strong but I have no doubt that you will persevere," she said feeling sorry for him. She knew it was Sophia's venom that caused this when she scratched him.

"I know that I once said that you cannot handle the demon's blood but you can, Alexander." She moved closer. Xander roared at her and broke free of one of his chains.

"Calm your storm! Take control of it. I know that you can, as I have," she said, then touched his head. His grey hair was thick and soft. Her touch instantly calmed him. Xander did not want to harm her. He could never hurt Danara. He overcame the evil inside of him and slowly transformed back into his human form.

"My love, you did it!" Anius said proudly.

"No, Xander did it. He is in control now," she said as the guards tended to Xander fetching his clothes. Danara finally turned to face her husband. Anius looked like he had aged. His hair was longer and he now had a full beard. He rushed into her arms kissing her passionately. She touched his beard and his face confused.

"I do not understand. What has happened to you?" she asked almost afraid to hear the answer.

"I got older." He laughed. "You . . . are just as beautiful as you always were. You don't know how long I've waited to see light in your eyes again." He cried tears of joy. "My love, you've been asleep for seven years."

After her initial shock, Anius took her to the stables to see Sophia. She was tending to Anius' warhorse, Splendor. Danara was still afraid to be around her daughter even after Josephine reassured her that all evil had been expunged during her seven-year slumber.

"I told them you would awaken today," Sophia said brushing a dying Splendor's mane for what she knew was the last time. Danara approached her alone while Anius and Josephine stayed close. Sophia wanted to leap into her mother's arms but she sensed her fear and maintained her composure. Danara cautiously sat down beside her and stroked Splendor gently. She too felt life leaving her husband's faithful horse.

"Splendor will be leaving this world soon. I told father not to be sad, she will be going to heaven," Sophia said sweetly. Splendor laid on a comfortable bed of hay taking her last breaths surrounded by love.

"You should not be sad either, mother, nor afraid. I cannot remember everything that occurred on the day of my birth, but the one thing that God has allowed me to remember about that day is you. You love me and you saved me," Sophia said as Splendor took her final breath. Danara struggled to find the words to say to her daughter.

"Is it alright if I touch your hand, mother?" Sophia asked politely. Danara was hesitant but she felt such a sense of peace near her. Sophia was very polite and spoke like she was wise beyond her years. Danara knew this was the influence of Anius and this warmed her heart.

"Yes, you may," Danara whispered. Sophia placed both of their hands over Splendor's heart.

"Splendor is dead now. She was very loyal and saved my father's life on many occasions. I want to give her what she desires most. Jesus said that if I believe, nothing is impossible for me. Do you have faith, mother?"

"Y-yes I do have faith," Danara answered.

"Jesus said we had to do this together. He told me that you would awaken today. I almost did not believe him because you have been asleep for so long but he never lies, and now you're awake. Just as he promised." Sophia smiled. Danara finally gazed upon her face. She had not aged since the last time that she saw her. She had the look of pure love in her green eyes.

"Fly, Splendor!" Sophia shouted. Danara's hands began to tingle. Splendor's body was illuminated by a bright yellow light. In an instant, she was gone.

"Come on, mother!" Sophia said excitedly. She led her mother out of the stables. Anius and Josephine followed.

"Father, look! It's what she always wanted!" Sophia was so excited. She jumped up and down as she held her mother and father's hand. Splendor flew over their heads with marvelous gold-tipped wings.

"We did it, mother!" she beamed. Danara was speechless. Splendor flew down landing in front of them. Sophia and Anius admired her soft gold and white wings.

"Jesus says she earned her wings, father, and he will ride her to the gates of heaven," Sophia said full of joy.

"Fly high, my friend. Until we meet again." Anius hugged Splendor as she neighed, then flew all around them leaving the trail of a glorious rainbow. She flew over them once more, then slowly ascended into the clouds.

"Thank you, Jesus!" Sophia shouted to the sky, then leaped into Danara's arms.

"Jesus says our love did that for Splendor," Sophia said laying her head on her mother's shoulder.

"Jesus . . . speaks to you?" Danara asked, trembling.

"Yes. He's always talking, mother. Sometimes he goes on and on." She giggled. Danara looked at Anius and Josephine with tears in her eyes.

"She speaks the truth," Anius confirmed.

"Jesus speaks to everyone, mother. People just need to open their hearts so they can hear him. He says that I am special and he reminds me every day. I am the only one that sees him. He says that is because I believe with my whole heart. Father taught me that." Danara hugged her daughter tightly.

"You . . . you trust in Jesus?" Danara's voice quivered.

"Of course I do, mother. I love and trust Jesus. He died on the cross for me as he did for you. I know there is nothing more honorable than sacrificing your life for another," she answered honestly.

"Your father has taught you well," Danara said still squeezing her.

"You taught me that, mother, when you sacrificed yourself to save me. For that, I will love and trust you forever, as I do our Lord and Savior," Sophia said as Danara sobbed. She suddenly felt exhausted as did her mother.

"I'm really sleepy father." She yawned.

"You should be my sweet girl. I know it took a lot of energy to do that for Splendor. I thank you both," he said, then took her into his arms. "It's time for a nap."

"Aw, but I can't sleep now. I don't want to leave mother," she said sadly.

"Don't worry, your mother is not going anywhere. How about we all lay down together?" Anius said carrying her back to the castle as he held his wife's hand.

Josephine parted from them to go and greet Karo and Aries whom she sensed had just returned with Aries' nephew, Dominick. He would now be living with his strict uncle so Aries could keep him out of trouble.

Anius took Sophia and Danara to their bedroom. It was kept intact just the way Danara remembered. She tucked Sophia into bed, then laid in between her and Anius. She felt drained and was afraid to fall asleep dreading she'd never again wake.

"You have been amazing with her, Anius. I cannot thank you enough."

"I should be thanking you, my love. The years without you would have been harder had you not left behind such a marvelous treasure. Sophia truly is the best part of all of us." He meant every word.

"Mother. I'm sorry that you were asleep for such a long time. I pray that when you sleep now, you will dream of us." Sophia yawned.

"That would make me so happy," Danara answered.

"Dream," Sophia whispered, then kissed her mother's right temple. Danara drifted into a peaceful sleep that she knew in her heart would not last as long as before. Sophia Grace was right. Danara dreamt of their seven years of peace and abundant love. She saw how they all stayed true to their word and kept Sophia safe and happy. Even Xander who was reluctant at first had learned to love her as his own blood. Josephine could not have loved Sophia more if she were her own daughter. Aries also had a hand in raising her teaching her about honor. Karo helped her hone her gifts and Anius taught her the most important lessons—to love and fear God, that no one comes before him except through Jesus Christ. He taught her to have compassion for others; never to use her gifts to harm, only to protect and defend. He taught her the sword in case she was ever without her power so she would still be able to defend herself. This also taught her discipline. The one thing he could not teach her was faith since that is of our own free will and it comes from the heart and soul. This lesson was instilled by her mother. She had unwavering faith in God when he worked through her to save Sophia. This made Danara's heart feel full and complete.

Several days of bliss had gone by. Danara spent her days with all of her loved ones making up for the lost time. She helped Xander control his affliction. Before Danara had awakened, Xander could not control his rage for the entire time that she was gone. He was plagued with having violent transformations only on full moons. With her guidance, he learned to control his power at will. She was impressed with how skilled Josephine became through the years. She evolved far beyond just controlling the elements. Her power was limitless. She was happy to see that although Josephine tried hard to hide her feelings, she and Karo still had much love for each other. They had been greatly tested especially during the time of Sophia's birth, but their love for each other survived. Danara parted some knowledge on Aries' nephew Dominick whom she felt was just immature at the age of twenty-one trying to find his way in the world. She had no doubt that Aries would turn him into an honorable man.

Danara spent her nights getting to know her husband's body and heart again. Her days were filled with wonder just witnessing how amazing Sophia was. There was no evil in her. She brought joy to everyone around her. She longed to be accepted by her people, but for her own safety, Anius never allowed outsiders near her, so when Elle Norah, wife of Simon Norah and dear friend of Aries' wife, came personally on behalf of the villagers in hopes to welcome Danara back and meet Sophia, her parents did not object. It was time.

Danara could not help but remember their wedding day as they marched through the streets with their people. The town was decorated in Sophia's favorite color, red. The villagers' homes were decorated with beautiful red ribbons. Their children threw rose petals at their feet as they marched to the town square.

"Do you remember our wedding march, old man?" Danara teased Anius.

"Ha, old, that's cute." He laughed.

"Of course, I do, my love. The happiest moment of my life was marrying you amongst God, our family, and our people. It feels good to be here with them again. Sophia is beyond overjoyed. I don't think she will ever want to go home. Look at how happy she is playing with other children," Anius said as they happily watched Sophia play hand in hand with the other children and danced until she was out of breath, then danced some more.

Xander was being entertained by the town's blacksmith who, in honor of the celebration, made him an impressive sword and shield as he did for their other great warrior Aries. Josephine and Karo drank wine and danced as she willed the wind to make the rose petals rain down on them. The town priest made his way through the crowd with Simon Norah to speak with their king and queen.

"We are truly honored by your presence," Simon Norah said happily shaking Anius' hand, then kissing Danara's.

"Thank you, Simon. It's been quite some time since I've seen you at court. How is your wife feeling? She says your baby is due soon. Many blessings to you and your family," Anius said really happy for them.

"Thank you, your highness. Blessings to yours as well. Yes, our baby is due any day now but that did not stop her from organizing this for you. She truly loves the queen and was delighted to meet Sophia," Simon answered. "Elle awaits us at the stables if you would oblige me for a moment. We have a gift for you. We heard of Splendor's passing and are sorry for your loss. The town has decided to gift you our finest stallion. We know that it cannot replace her but would be honored if you accepted." Simon bowed humbly.

"Simon, I am touched. I thank you all but—" Anius began, Danara interrupted.

"No buts, they would be offended if you declined. It is very kind of you, my husband accepts," she insisted. Anius could not resist her smile.

"Well, you heard my wife. Lead the way, Simon," Anius said, then kissed his wife's cheek and left with Simon.

"It is wonderful to see you on your feet, my queen," Priest said walking with Danara toward the church. Sophia played with the children in front of the church steps as her mother kept a watchful eye on her.

"State your business, Priest," she said firmly. She knew he wanted something from her but since she no longer possessed the demon's power, she could not read his thoughts. She and Priest had never gotten along. She was of the same religion as her mother Annalise, Baptist. Anius' family and even Danara's father were Catholic. Priest felt offended that she never converted, but for her, it never mattered what she was labeled as it was about belief. Since she was a small child, she had always loved and served God. Anius respected this and did not force his religion on Sophia. He let it be Sophia's choice of what religion to follow and she chose the same religion as her mother, Baptist, because that is what she felt in her heart. Priest was insulted especially since Anius would still seek his guidance and trusted his council in many things, but on the matter of Sophia, he did not budge. Danara was appreciative of this beyond words and nothing that Priest had to tell her would change that.

"I owe you an apology. Not once in your seven-year slumber did I visit you. I was wrong for that and I am sorry," he genuinely apologized.

"No worries. As you can see, I survived without you, Priest. It was the God we both serve that saved me. I hold no ill will toward you. We have different religions but serve the same God and he is a God of love. He loves all and accepts all. There should be no friction between us. We are all his children. He doesn't love you anymore for being Catholic nor love me any less for being Baptist. We should show our innocent children the right way to do things and that is in unity." Danara smiled as she saw the joy on all of the children's faces as they played with Sophia. Priest was taken aback by her words. He expected anger from her, not understanding. He cleared his throat, searching for the right response.

"When the Lord came to me last night and told me that your heart had changed and to accept you into his church, this was not what I expected. I know you do not care to step foot into the church that rejected you but I welcome you to pray with me in God's house with open arms," he said kissing her hand, then took her by the arm as they walked together up the church steps. He stepped inside, Danara hesitated. She looked inside. The church benches were beautifully decorated with her favorite white lilies. She looked back at her family enjoying this moment being accepted by their people. This was already more than she ever dreamed. She would never ask God for more. She regretted that there was a time that she slaughtered the friends and family of the same people that now forgave and accepted her. She had never been able to forgive herself for that but if Jesus was now welcoming her into his church, this had to mean that it was time. God had truly given her everything her heart desired and so much more. She struggled to take the first step into the church. Emotion came over her and tears fell down her face.

"The choice to come inside is yours whenever you are ready. You are apprehensive because you know the end of your pain is inside. Forgiveness and salvation await you at God's altar, but you have to take the steps and it is hard. It is not supposed to be easy but you know as I do that it is necessary. Princess Sophia is welcome as well. The Lord has told me who her true father is and she is still loved by God and all of us. I welcome you both into his house," Priest said assuredly.

"Mother! Come play with us," Sophia called out from the bottom of the church stairs.

"In a minute. There is something I must do first," Danara answered smiling.

"Join us, Princess Sophia," Priest said as Danara took a step inside the church. Sophia eagerly ran up the stairs, took her mother's hand, then she too walked inside of the church. Priest quietly closed the doors behind them.

The sound of the church doors closing hurt Josephine's ears. She looked around for her dear friend Danara although her heart already knew exactly where she was. She suddenly stopped dancing with Karo and looked at all the faces smiling back at her. She put down her glass of wine. An uneasy feeling came over her.

"Go find Anius," she whispered to Karo.

"What? Why? Woman, you have that look in your eyes. There is nothing to be worried about," Karo said trying to ease her troubled mind.

Josephine suddenly felt a horrible pain in the pit of her stomach. She left Karo where he stood, then walked toward the church. The children who were playing with Sophia stood in front of the church staring at it. When Josephine got close, the children all turned in unison, then formed a circle around her laughing and dancing. She saw Anius at her far left with Simon and Elle Norah at the stables. Xander was at her far-right at the blacksmiths flirting with his daughter Talia as she placed the armor specially made on him. Karo joined Josephine, then the children surrounded him too and continued dancing around them.

"This is exactly why you don't drink. It makes you paranoid. I see worry all over your face Josephine. All is well. We've had seven glorious years of peace. Danara is back. There is nothing to worry about. If there was anything wrong, we would know," Karo said pulling her close. His words fell on deaf ears. Every instinct in her body was screaming. She looked down at the children dancing around her and Karo. For a quick moment, they all had horns protruding out of their heads. All of their hands had blood on them. Josephine knew instantly that the blood on their hands was her own.

"Simon and Elle Norah, you have truly honored me. This horse is superb," Anius said inspecting the black beauty.

"You deserve our very best," Simon said as he drank with his wife Elle.

"I think I should sit for a moment," Elle said sweating as her stomach cramped. Anius and Simon helped her sit on a nearby stool.

"This child is intent on ruining the festivities. It must be a rambunctious boy. He is just as naughty as his father." She giggled as the pain subsided.

"Have you chosen a name yet?" Anius asked handing her some water.

"Not yet. We want so desperately for this one to be a boy. As you know, we already have two lovely daughters. Simon wants a boy to pass down all he knows. We couldn't allow ourselves to believe it is in fact a boy and give him a name. I . . . I had a son two years ago but he died after birth. I would give anything to be able to give my husband a son," Elle Norah said sadly.

"May I?" Anius asked for permission to touch her stomach. She agreed. He touched the top of her stomach. It was hard.

"I pray that God blesses you with a healthy, honorable son. I am very sorry for your tremendous loss. God has made this one especially strong. Simon can also pass down all he knows to your daughters. I understand the need to have a son but always let your children know how loved and valuable they are." Elle Norah was touched by his words. Anius felt her baby move.

"There you are. Elle and Simon, you should choose a name fast. I can assure you this child is a boy and he is on his way." Anius smiled.

"You are too kind, my king," Elle Norah cried.

"A-are you certain?" Simon asked anxiously.

"God has just showed me the face of your boy. I do not wish to scare you but your son is in distress. Fear not, Danara had a similar issue with Sophia. She was turned around and I had to cut her out myself. Trust in the Lord. Your son will be fine. Have faith, Elle Norah. Be brave for your boy," Anius said, then immediately her pain worsened.

"Simon, get my guards. We should get her to the castle. I'll have the royal physician deliver him," Anius said, then Simon quickly left. Elle Norah was in so much pain she could not even scream. Blood poured out of her body. Anius felt for a second that he was reliving Sophia's birth. He knew that if he did not deliver the boy right now, he would indeed perish like his brother before him. He removed his sword, told her to have faith, then sliced her wound open. Her son came into the world smiling. Anius took him into his arms, then severed the umbilical cord. The child looked at Anius with eyes fresh from heaven.

"You definitely look like a Pascal," he said, then handed Elle Norah her son and healed her wound with heaven's flame.

"My king, I do not know how to even begin to thank you." She sobbed with her son finally in her arms. "What is the meaning of this name?" she asked.

"I am not entirely sure, to be honest. It is significant with Easter. In Hebrew, I believe Pascal means Passover. One thing I am certain of is that Lucifer had his grip on your son. He would've taken this one's life too but God said *no*. So, the spirit of death passed over your son and will undoubtedly claim the life of another. I promise you that your son is protected. He has the eyes of destiny and he will do amazing things in God's honor. Choose a good name for him. God has shown me that one day, his name will be written in the stars," Anius said as Simon returned with four men and an ax.

"Simon, you missed all the excitement. Come and meet your son," Anius said happily. Elle Norah continued to sob.

"Why do you cry? Your boy is here and safe. I assure you he will be strong," Anius reassured her.

"I cry because I am sorry my king," she sobbed hysterically.

"Sorry for what Elle?" Anius asked concerned. Before she could answer, Simon came forward with his ax raised high in the air. Anius turned around just before Simon struck the ax down beheading his king. Pascal began to scream in his mother's arms. The child could see what others could not. When his father struck the honorable king down, instead of blood pouring out where the king's head once was, the baby saw a glorious blue flame that was so beautiful and powerful that it immediately blinded the son of Simon and Elle Norah.

"Mother, I don't like it here," Sophia said to Danara as they walked down the church aisle.

"Honestly, I never really liked it here, either," Danara said as she walked holding Sophia's hand. Her throat began to feel itchy and she started to cough.

"Mother! Mother!" Sophia cried out afraid. She looked around for Jesus. He was not with her.

"Priest, fetch my mother some water at once," she ordered.

"You heard the princess. Our queen needs some water," Priest said with his knees bent before the statue of Mary, the mother of Jesus. Six men came in through the church's back door.

"S-Sophia, Anius is dead. They killed your father," Danara said choking.

"No mother, my father is not dead, you are wrong. Why would you think such a thing? I'll take you to him, you will see," she said helping her mother stand. "Get out of my way!" Sophia shouted at the men. She searched for what could be causing her mother to fall ill. She sensed something close. She looked up and saw lilies all over the church ceiling. She noticed the lilies when they first walked in, they were all over the benches. She thought to herself, *why would there be so many?*. She picked up one of the white lilies and immediately realized they were not lilies. White color smudged on her fingers exposing the flowers' true purple color. These were verbena. They were tricked. Danara could no longer breathe. She fell to the ground. Three of the men quickly approached grabbing Danara. Sophia would not let her go. She wanted to fight but fear crippled her. The three men dragged Danara's body to the stoup that held the holy water. It too was filled with the verbena flower.

"Release her!" Sophia shouted as she ran toward her mother. The other three men yanked Sophia from behind, then placed a cloth over her face suffocating her until she passed out.

When Sophia awoke, her mother's body was beside her. Danara's wrist were both slashed from the bottom of her wrist to her inner elbow. There were bite marks all around the cuts. Danara's face was unrecognizable. The holy water tainted with the verbena melted her skin.

"Mother," she whispered afraid. She placed her hand on her mother's chest. She was still alive.

"P-princess Sophia, this is not what I wanted," Priest pleaded.

"Lucifer said we had to obey. He said Danara would kill us all when she awakened and that he would protect us. He informed us of all your weaknesses and how to fool you. But this . . . this was not right. I did not wish for King Anius to die. The-king-is-dead. I should have warned him," Priest sobbed.

"You betrayed God for Lucifer. Nothing I do to you will be worse than his wrath. The devil you chose has betrayed you as you knew he would. You taught your congregation to fear him and trust in God yet you do not practice what you have preached. You do not deserve to wear the cloth," Sophia said, then got up and ripped off his white collar. Priest fell at her feet.

"Please forgive me I was weak-spirited. I only wanted to protect the people from Danara," he cried.

"You only wanted to help yourself. Had you turned to God, he would have delivered you. I will come for you after I've destroyed the evil you have unleashed. The villagers drank from my mother. Now they are all infected with Lucifer's blood. You have no idea what you have done," Sophia said, then returned to her mother. She tried not to focus on the death of her father because her mother needed her now. Her heart deeply ached. She placed her hands over her mother's heart. She was only able to heal her face.

"This is God's will. I cannot heal you. God has abandoned us. Jesus has left me. He promised that he would never leave me." Sophia cried as she cradled her mother in her arms.

"God will *never* abandon us," Danara said now able to speak. "You may not see Jesus but he is *always* watching over you. We still live because that is God's will. Never stop trusting in him. Promise me. Your father taught you well, remember all that he put in you. Anius is with God now. He dedicated his life to him. Everything he believed in was true," Danara said wiping her daughter's tears.

"I promise mother. I will *always* trust in God and our Lord. *Always!*" Sophia promised. They looked up at the church doors when they heard footsteps approaching.

"Mother, we have to leave," Sophia said anxiously.

"Go out through the back. I will hold them off," Priest said wanting to help them.

"I cannot stand. The damage already done cannot be reversed. They will come back for my blood until they have completely drained me. They will spread evil throughout this world. I cannot allow that. Sophia, do you understand what I must do?" Danara said weakly. Sophia nodded, then sobbed in her mother's arms.

"You must find Josephine. She will keep you safe," Danara said gently to her daughter.

"My queen. Josephine is dead." Priest's voice quivered as he uttered the words.

"She is not!" Danara said sternly.

"I . . . I saw it with my own eyes. Josephine tried to protect Alexander and the others but she was overcome. The villagers' children stabbed her, then they set her on fire. They said she was a witch and had to burn. Alexander was trapped in the silver armor

Talia and her father made. He could not transform or help her. When the people attacked them, Josephine created a . . . I have never seen anything like it. It was a black hole that consumed half of the village. It pulled Xander and Karo in. Most of the children were also pulled in. Josephine massacred half of the village before they plunged King Anius' sword into her skull and she finally fell." Priest shuttered as he explained. Josephine's power was frightening. He was not sorry that she was dead. He was relieved.

"Where is she now?" Danara asked.

"They took her body away after they burned her. I do not know where," he answered truthfully.

"Queen Danara. Thank God you are still alive!" Dominick said at the church door. He was battered and bloody. Danara knew that he fought to defend her family, even after Aries was killed. The villagers stabbed Aries in the back over twenty times. They knew that even at his ripe age of seventy-two, he was still a threat and would not have gone down easily.

"Dominick, help her," Sophia ordered. He quickly obliged.

"Do not touch me," Danara protested but it was too late. Dominick touched her arm and his eyes immediately turned black. Her blood seeped into the open wounds on his hands infecting him at once. His body fell backward as he clutched his head.

*"No! I will not kill her!"* Dominick shouted. Lucifer was now in his head, ordering him to kill Danara. He fought but the evil was too great and overpowered him. Dominick was not a spiritual man nor was he a follower of Lucifer. Since he believed in no God, he was not spiritually equipped to defend himself against Lucifer's attack with faith and God's word. He arose, then leaped toward Danara. Sophia raised her hand striking him with a strong magnetic pulse sending his body flying out of the church doors. Sophia fell into her mother's lap. Her body was exhausted from trying to heal her mother and now defending her from Dominick.

"I am sorry, mother. I am not strong like you," she said faintly.

"You are stronger than all of us, my child. Thank you for protecting me. It is my turn to protect you now." Danara kissed her.

"Mother you can't, you will die. I can feel it. Please don't leave me again," she cried. Dominick came crawling back into the church flat on his stomach. He forced his body to remain on the ground as long as he could. He truly did not want to do Lucifer's bidding and kill his queen. Still, he arose, then began to move toward them.

"Please help us, Jesus. You promised that you would always be there to save me. I need you now. I will not let Lucifer have her. I will die for her." Sophia prayed and believed that the Lord could hear her.

"What . . . what is that?" Danara said startled as the room was suddenly filled with what looked like white snow falling down all around them.

"Mother, they're here!" Sophia said excitedly.

"Who? Who is here?" Danara asked.

"The angels!" Sophia answered eagerly.

Dominick roared, then ran toward them. He immediately fell. Priest looked on, confused. Dominick looked as though he was struck and was forcefully being held down but no one was there. He clawed at the floor but could not move.

"It's Jesus! He came back for me," Sophia said feeling her energy return. Danara saw her Lord for the first time. Jesus had his right foot on Dominick's back. Danara could not see his face because he was surrounded by light. The light slowly dimmed, then Danara saw that there were twelve angels with him. They were all women.

"Thank you, Jesus," Sophia said humbly.

Jesus dragged Dominick down the aisle by one arm, then placed him at Danara's feet. She could no longer see the Lord but she knew that he was there. Priest could not see Jesus nor the angels. He understood it was because he was not worthy. He bowed and remained with his knees bent, face flat on the floor, and arms stretched out in front of him. He did not speak nor move from that position. He knew without seeing that he was in the presence of the Lord.

"P-please my queen . . . forgive me," Dominick begged Danara at her feet.

"God wants you to live even though you do not believe in him. You are now infected with Lucifer's blood. I would kill you had he not instructed me to do otherwise," she said sternly.

"I am so sorry, I tried to fight the urge. I don't know what happened but . . . I no longer hear Lucifer in my head." He begged his queen to forgive him. She was not moved by his tears or words but she knew Jesus severed Lucifer's connection to him. "I will never betray you or Princess Sophia again. Please believe me," Dominick cried.

"It is fortunate that you are the blood of Aries, God favors him. Aries is with God and my husband now," she said, then looked upon the angels.

"Dominick, you will take Sophia to safety. Whatever she needs, you will provide as long as you are on earth. The day you betray her, *I will come for you.*" Danara grabbed his throat. "You will betray her. God has shown me that you will one day and when you do, I will come from the bowels of hell to claim your soul. This I promise you Dominick, blood of Aries." Her eyes shined emerald green staring through his soul. He felt chills throughout his body. She frightened him to his core because he believed she meant exactly what she said and that one day, she would come to drag his soul to hell.

"Leave us now and await her outside," Danara ordered. He quickly obeyed and left. She leaned back and suddenly felt no pain.

"You were murdered for loving another woman," Danara said pointing at one of the angels. "Your lover no longer lives but she is not with you in heaven. She burns because she took her own life. She was heartbroken after your death. You were taught since you were young that God hates you for loving another woman yet you still believed in him so he welcomed you with open arms when your time here had ended. He made you one of his elite warrior angels for your loyalty and belief. Because of his extraordinary love, you still hold on to hope. You believe that you will see your love again. You know firsthand that anything is possible with God. Your belief in him touched him. For this, he made your angel name Hope. When I see the love of your life, I will tell her what your heart has told mine," Danara said causing Hope to cry tears of joy.

"Thank you, Danara," Hope said raising a closed fist, then placing it over her heart.

"You were killed for being different," Danara said to another angel. "You were born a man but you felt trapped in your own body and transitioned into a woman. Your family abandoned you and told you God has abandoned you too but you believed and trusted that the God of love could never hate. Your own parents tossed you out yet God accepted you as a woman and did not change you when he welcomed you into his heaven. Not because he felt he made a mistake creating you as a man but because he accepted you in the form that you accepted yourself and allowed you to have what you truly desired. You have been spat on, beaten, ridiculed, and forsaken from the church you were raised in yet you still held on to your faith and belief in him. For that, he made your angel name Faith because you never lost yours. You changed his heart and he honored you for that." Faith was speechless as tears of sparkling diamonds fell down her face.

"You! Come forward. Do not hide your scars from me." Danara pointed at the one angel that would not look her in the eye.

"You are Carmen. You are so special to God that he did not change your name," Danara said, then Carmen came forward. "Your angel name would have been Honor. You never felt you deserved it. On earth, your husband tormented you and beat you down daily. He caused turmoil in your family and did not allow you to have a relationship with your own mother. You would communicate with her through the walls of your home and sneak over to her apartment when your husband was not around since your mother lived right next door. You were so broken down mentally, physically, and emotionally that you accepted this. You feared for the life of your two daughters so you stayed with their father until he destroyed you. Your love for God was what kept you going but even when he accepted you into heaven, you never felt worthy. You still believed that you were worthless because that is how your husband, your love, treated you for so long. When Lucifer attacked heaven, you were the first to defend God and for that, Lucifer scarred you," Danara said looking at Carmen's face. Lucifer had disfigured her when he struck her with his bloody hand. His poisonous blood melted her left eye and the entire left side of her face, making it difficult for her to speak.

"You never asked God to heal you nor did you complain of your scars. You wore them like a badge of honor and will stand for God for all time. Lucifer did not break you. When God made you his most favored warrior angel, he could not easily decide on your new name.

You are so special to him that he left you as Carmen, his charm." Danara placed her bloody hand over Carmen's scars.

"God told you that you would see me today and the only thing that could heal you is Lucifer's blood. He told you I would heal you and all you had to do was ask. You would not ask this of me because you know the cost. You would rather stay in agony forever because that was the price you gladly paid to defend our God. You know that Lucifer's blood flows through me and with it, you are now healed," Danara said, and it was so. Carmen grabbed her hand at first. She did not want Danara to hurt herself to heal her but it was done. God did not ask this of Danara. She chose this with her own free will knowing it would kill her and send her damned soul to hell.

"You will not live in agony for another moment because of Lucifer," Danara said sincerely. Carmen clutched her face, then spoke for the first time in many years.

"Sweet, strong, faithful, and brave Danara. I pray I find the right words to express how much I appreciate your sacrifice yet I wish you had not done this for me. Lucifer will punish you dearly for helping me," Carmen said wrapping her wings around Danara.

"I do not fear him. Whatever he does, I will never regret helping you. You were the first to fight back when Lucifer foolishly thought he could kill God. You reminded him of what loyalty was. I am honored to have helped the bravest woman I have ever come across," Danara said as Carmen held her for a moment longer, then had to join her fellow warriors.

They were alerted to the commotion just outside the church. Lucifer's minions were now there. Dominick was fighting them keeping them from entering the church. God's warrior angels left to aid him. Only Carmen remained.

"They've come for Sophia. Lucifer knows you are weakened. We will not let him take her," Carmen vowed.

"Thank you, Carmen," Danara said, then felt a terrible pain in her chest near her heart.

"Jesus, why won't you heal her?" Sophia asked. The Lord did not answer.

"That is not God's will," Danara said staring at her daughter. "Listen to me my amazing, beautiful girl. You are as special as those warrior angels. God needs you to live. I know I must sacrifice myself for that to happen," Danara said, then cried out in pain. Her body was slowly dying. She had used the last of her blood to heal Carmen.

"This can't be, mother! If you take your life, you will be damned as Hope's love is. God does not spare the damned no matter how noble their death. You know that. That is his absolute law. Life is his most precious gift to us. Lucifer will torture you for all eternity. God will not deliver you. Not even for helping Carmen," Sophia cried hysterically.

"You know many things but you do not know God's intent or his plan. Remember that his warrior Faith changed his heart. Always remember that Anius chose to love you. God brought us all together. You don't understand what that means now but you will one day and it will change everything for you. I do not fear the evil that awaits me. God is with me always, wherever I go. This is my choice. If I asked God to spare me, he would, but the only way to keep you safe is to do this. You must never forget those who sacrificed themselves for you or the miracles that God performed so that you live. Lucifer will try to poison your mind, make you forget our love, make you feel worthless. His strength comes from our fear. So, I need you to be fearless. I am not angry with God nor should you be. He gave me you and I rejected you at first not knowing you would be my greatest blessing. I am eternally grateful to God for you, for Anius, for all of you. He gave you and I these blessed few days so I could see how truly magnificent and important you are. Always put God first. *Never* doubt his love or else Lucifer wins," Danara said as her pain intensified. Priest could hear the agony in her voice. He was deeply ashamed of himself and disgusted with the part he played in all of this. He kept his head down and prayed for her.

"Mother, if he takes you away, I fear for what I will do. I've always had Father, Josephine, and the others to guide me. I know I cannot survive alone and that the evil took hold of me before. I'm not strong enough to fight Lucifer. I don't know why he hunts me but I am certain that he will never stop. How could you leave me alone? I will not be safe without you." Sophia was overcome with grief and fear.

"*Enough*! I know this is hard but I need you to be brave. There are angels out there fighting for you. Our family happily died for you because you are that important. The sacrifices made for you were worth it. You don't understand or believe that but you will in time. You will be brave for me right now, as I am doing all I can to be strong for you. Do you believe that I will see you again? Do you believe in God's unwavering love?" Although Danara was suffering, Sophia heard her incredible strength in her voice. She knew this came from her mother's faith.

"Yes, mother, I believe in God's love. It saved us once before. I believe he will reunite us again," Sophia said no longer crying. Danara felt as if her body was splitting in two. Carmen came forward and stood behind Sophia.

"*I love you* with my entire heart. I give you my last bit of strength and will all of my power and love to pass over to you. When things get dark, I pray that you remember the light. I will do the same. You are my light, Sophia Grace," Danara said, then her head fell back, her mouth opened, and all of the souls she had ever consumed left her body and entered Sophia's causing her to immediately fall into a deep sleep. Carmen took Sophia into her capable arms.

"I see hell's flame. I can feel its heat but I no longer feel pain," Danara said, then Carmen brought Sophia to her so she could kiss her daughter one last time.

"You do not feel pain because you are in the arms of our Lord and Savior Jesus Christ." Carmen smiled.

"I have faith that I will see you again, Carmen. I trust that you will keep my precious girl safe. I will find a way to keep Lucifer at bay. He will never step foot on earth as long as I am with him in hell. When Sophia forgets, please remind her that I love her," Danara said as she began to fade.

"You have my word. He will never claim Sophia. I swear on my honor, I will never let her forget your love and sacrifice. I will remind her in every possible way, Queen." Carmen bowed. Before Danara faded, she heard a voice speak to her.

"*Be strong and of good courage, do not fear nor be afraid of them; for the Lord your God is the one that goes with you,*" said the Lord.

When Carmen looked up, Jesus and Danara were gone. Carmen did as God instructed her. The twelve warrior angels easily destroyed Lucifer's minions, then they escorted Sophia and Dominick to safety. When Sophia was safe, the angels returned to heaven.

Sophia slept for three days. Dominick cared for her as he promised the angels he would. On the fourth day, she awoke. She never spoke, only prayed in her heart, and fasted until God sent her a vision on the seventh day.

"Acts 3 verse 19," Priest began. It was Sunday and although there was chaos all around him, he still held church service. This was all he knew. Only ten of the villagers showed, three were children. Everyone else was dead or hiding from the others that were infected by Danara's blood when they took it from her.

"Repent then and turn to God, so that your sins may be wiped out, that times of refreshing may come from the Lord." Priest read the passage as his voice echoed in the nearly empty church. "We must all repent for our sins. Our fears led us to trust in the devil himself. We do not deserve to draw breath yet God still allows it," said Priest.

"Maybe we are alive because we did the right thing. As far as I'm concerned, Lucifer kept his word. The queen is dead and I still live," a villager named William said laughing.

"No, William. We are wrong for what we've done. You are here because you too believe that and you are just as afraid and ashamed as we are. We must humble ourselves before the Lord," Priest answered. William stood up.

"I don't need to hear this, especially not from you, Priest. I'm not even sure why I came," William said, then left.

"Daniel 9 verse 9. The Lord our God is merciful and forgiving, even though we have rebelled against him," Priest continued. William ran back inside the church.

"She has returned," William yelled afraid.

When Priest saw the look of fear on his face, he knew it was Sophia he spoke of and that she had returned to exact her revenge. She stood at the church door in an all-black dress that dragged on the floor. Her face was not visible because she wore a long black hood that covered her head and face entirely. Still, all knew it was her. Sophia was not the girl Priest saw just seven days ago. Her innocence was gone and they were all responsible for that. She now understood true pain. She was no longer their princess. She was the bringer of death.

"Evil cannot enter God's holy house," William shouted at Sophia confidently.

"You are here. Are you not evil? You played a part in the demise of your own kingdom. You are responsible for the death of your king and queen. Besides, William, these are just walls and windows. It is faith that keeps evil out. Neither you nor Priest who has misguided you have any," Sophia said without emotion, then stepped into the church. Her words were true and hit them all like a mighty blow.

"Please, Sophia, have mercy on my child. Whatever is my fate, I accept it. I only ask that you let her go," a frightened mother pleaded. Sophia looked at her daughter who was not much younger than she was. She touched her face gently.

"You will all be given the same amount of mercy you showed my family," she answered coldly, then closed the church doors trapping them inside. She stood before the statue of the Virgin Mary, then removed her hood. "After all you've done, do you really think that I would spare you, hypocrites?" She laughed. "You do not even follow your own scripture. You worship false idols," she said causing the statue of Mary to shatter.

"How dare you desecrate the house of God," Priest shouted.

"It was just a statue." Sophia smiled. "You worship her yet what has she done for you?" Sophia asked, then stood at the pulpit.

"She is the mother of Jesus Christ!" Priest screamed so fiercely his body shook.

"She was a vessel. God could have chosen anyone," she preached.

"Yes, God could have and he did. He chose Mary just as he chose Danara to be your mother and . . . Anius your father," Priest said calming down.

"Ah! Yes! Your king and queen. Where are their statues?" Sophia asked.

"They do not deserve to have statues in the house of God. They did not die on the cross for us, Jesus did!" he shouted.

"Exactly! Neither did Mary!" Sophia shouted pointing at the broken statue of the Virgin Mary. "I mean, no disrespect against our Lord's mother. I admire her courage and the unbreakable faith that she had in God. I had to address that because from the moment I stepped into your precious church, all I hear is 'Mary please save us, Mary, don't let her kill my children'. I find that incredibly offensive because I do not hear Mary's voice. It is not she who pleads for your life. No one comes to the Father except through Jesus Christ. It is Jesus who pleads for your miserable lives," Sophia said staring directly at Priest.

"*Blasphemer!* You do not hear our prayers. You do not hear the voice of God. You are not worthy of such a miracle. This is the work of evil," Priest shouted at her even though he knew deep inside that she was right. He was ashamed to admit in front of his followers that he, their priest of many years, did not hear the voice of God. He was unable to see Jesus before when he felt his powerful presence yet Jesus not only spoke to the daughter of Lucifer but he also protected her as did God and his angels.

"You are not worthy of leading. You lost your way long ago, Priest. You are spiritually weak. Your weakness let the devil into your mind and made you molest the innocent. It was your wickedness that led me here. I prayed to our God for four days after the murder of my entire family. I prayed for a sign or a vision. Today, God answered my prayers. He showed me a sign. What the King of kings showed me was you, Priest. You and fire," Sophia said and grabbed Priest by his white-collar, then dragged him to the door. When the door opened, all the people could see outside was the fire. The very ground the church once stood upon was gone. The people gasped as Sophia walked out of the church and into the fire. She remained unburned.

"You are a coward, Priest. Lucifer came to you knowing you would help him because that is how far removed you are from the very church you stand in. You had a choice to make and you chose Lucifer. Where-is -he-now?" she shouted. "You are a worthless scum. I want nothing more than to crush your skull and devour your soul but God has asked a favor of me. Would you walk through the fire for the God you have forgotten.?" she asked taking one step back.

"Don't do it, Priest, she lies. She is evil. We know that you would never molest our children. Sophia is the devil!" the villagers shrieked. Sophia was unfazed by their words. She took six more steps backward. Still, the fire did not burn her. Priest began to cry because nothing that she said was a lie.

"Stop it! Please do not pity me . . . Sophia is telling the truth. I . . . I did abuse your children. I am not worthy of leading you. I do deserve to burn," he said with his head down in shame. The villagers instantly began to attack him kicking, punching, and spitting on him.

"*Enough!*" Sophia shouted when she was satisfied with his beating. The people looked up at her and saw that she had all of their children across the fire beside her. Some of their parents tried to leap into the fire but she did not permit it. Sophia heard the villagers praying to Mary again in her mind. "You just don't get it. The Virgin Mary, God rest her precious soul, cannot save you. Jesus is the way, the truth, and the life!" Sophia screamed at them. They all fell silent now even more afraid because she proved that she did in fact hear their prayers. They knew then that God did send her and it was not for her to help them.

"Walk through the fire, Priest, and I will spare them all," Sophia promised.

"I . . . I can't. I am afraid. I don't want to burn," he sobbed.

"I knew you did not have it in you," Sophia said, then instantly moved beside him leaving the children alone in the fire. She forced him to stand.

"I did what you asked of me. I gave him a choice. Once again, he chose wrong," Sophia said looking to the sky. She grabbed Priest's arm and meant to throw him in the fire but she suddenly stopped. Jesus stood before her and told her to repeat his words exactly. She turned to Priest with tears in her eyes and recited what she didn't know at the time were Anius' final words that he said to Priest the night before his death.

"Walk by faith, not by sight," she said, then without hesitation, Priest walked through the fire and reached the children leaving behind a road made of stone footsteps. It created a path leading outside of their town which was now completely engulfed in fire.

"Follow the path and never return," Sophia instructed the villagers. They thanked her, then left.

"Thank you, merciful God," Priest shouted to the sky. "Thank you, Sophia. I know that Anius sent you and I thank him as well. He came to me the day before he died. His faith was shaken, he did not know what to do. He struggled with allowing outsiders around you. He was deeply troubled as if he felt his end coming. I could not counsel him. I struggled with my own faith so instead, he counseled me. He told me to trust in God and to walk by faith, not by sight. I was too weak to heed his wise words. He was a great king and he still is even in death." Priest bowed his head.

"My father was and still is a great man but God sent me to test you and it was Jesus who asked me to spare you. He led me here. He told me to recite those words to you. God sent the Lord to me on your behalf. He knew Jesus was the only one I would listen to," she said honestly.

"Why? Forgive me, I am profoundly grateful. I just need to understand," Priest asked.

"God has his reasons for sparing you. If he would have sent my father to plead for you, the sight of his face would have reminded me of what you all did to him and that would've angered me so that you would already be dead. He sent Jesus because there is no one I respect more. He died for me. His pain is greater than any I've known or ever will know and he did not deserve any of it. I know that I am a monster yet he treats me like an equal. He loves me as my father did and as my mother learned too. I do not deserve his love and neither do you. The only reason you did not burn when you walked through the fire was that Jesus carried you on his shoulders. The path that your followers are now on lead them to safety which is the stone footprints of our Savior," she said, then Priest sobbed like never before.

All that she said was the fact. Priest had forgotten God's sacrifice. He abused young boys. He lied, he sinned, and he worshipped false idols. He did betray his congregation and let Lucifer in yet God still forgave him and used a person created from pure evil to save him. This was the God he once knew and would never again forget.

"There is one more thing I require from you, Priest," she said.

"Yes, anything," he answered eagerly to assist her.

"Take me to Josephine."

Priest took her back into the church and through the back door. She extinguished some of the fire exposing the lake.

"After they burned her, the villagers that remained still feared her. They did not rest easy until she was at the bottom of the lake," Priest said ashamed. Sophia laughed out loud.

"God truly has a sense of humor. I spared you but Josephine will definitely slaughter you all for this. She hates water. She had to drown countless times before she learned to wield it and now you, idiots, have made the water her tomb. You are a dead man, Priest." She giggled. He stared at her with his mouth open in shock.

"I . . . I assure you. She is dead," he stuttered.

"You, fools, really think you murdered her. Ha! You mortals could never. I know many things but I still have not learned what Josephine truly is. One thing I am certain of is that she will only leave earth by God's hand. She serves a higher purpose and nothing will get in the way of that," Sophia said, then willed Josephine's body out of the lake with her mind and placed her in front of them. She still had Anius' sword in her skull. None of the villagers had been able to remove it.

"I almost feel bad for what she is going to do to you for this, even Jesus is looking away," Sophia said seriously, no longer laughing.

"My Lord, please do not forsake me," Priest begged looking around searching for the Lord's presence.

"I am just toying with you, Priest. Jesus would never turn his back on you," she said and he let out a sigh of relief. "He did, however, have to leave for a moment to escort the villagers to safety. So, you're kind of on your own right now." She giggled, then willed Josephine's shackles to release her. She took hold of her father's sword and easily pulled it out of Josephine's skull awakening her instantly. Josephine sat up, coughing up water.

"You asses could not remove the sword because it is mine now. Only I can wield it," she said, then her father's sword took its position floating in the air behind her in a defensive stance ready to attack whatever came close to her. There it would always remain. Priest could no longer see it for it was now invisible to the human eye and could only be seen by those with spiritual eyes. Josephine arose slowly. With each passing second, her wounds quickly healed. She approached Priest as he clutched his rosary and prayed. His hands shook terribly.

"Why does he still live? He knew what they were planning. You are responsible for the deaths of my brothers, my love Karo, Aries, and Danara, my beloved sister." Water poured out of her mouth as she spoke. "Of all the places, you put me in the fucking lake!!" Josephine shouted. Words would not dare part from Priest's lips, not even to apologize.

"Aunt Josephine, I understand your anger," Sophia began. Josephine realized that they were surrounded by fire. Everything in their kingdom was destroyed by the flames, except for the church.

"Sophia must have saved you for me because there is no other way that she would let you live," Josephine said as her glare not only made his hair stand up. All of the hair on his body left him.

"Josephine, God says Priest is not to be harmed," Sophia said in the calmest tone she could muster up.

"I say he dies!" Josephine answered still approaching him.

"You are my father's blood. I do not want to hurt you so I tell you again. *God said no*! I will enforce that even if I have to put you back into that lake myself," Sophia said undeniably.

"Then it will be God's lightning bolt that I use to strike Priest down," Josephine screamed causing the sky to rumble and clouds to disperse. A bolt of lightning shot from the sky and Josephine aimed it at Priest. Anius' sword that was now Sophia's intercepted the bolt before it hit Priest forming an X in front of him.

"God says that this is his symbol. The X means any man, woman, or child that he has marked with this is his treasure. This signifies a soul that was lost but now has been found and saved by his grace. This cannot be challenged, widow," Sophia said as Josephine's anger began to wither.

"What did you call me?" Josephine asked, trembling.

"God said you were married in secret to Karo near the oak trees where you found the verbena flower just days before my mother awakened. You hid your love for Karo since I used it against you and nearly killed the two of you after my birth. You both said your secret vows only to each other. God heard you and acknowledges you as Karo's widow. He promises that one day, you will be reunited with the love of your life and God will marry you both himself in heaven." Josephine's legs buckled and she dropped to the ground. Sophia joined her.

"It was not easy for me to spare him either but God promised me vengeance. We must destroy those that now possess Lucifer's blood. They are already spreading his evil. Will you help me?" Sophia asked.

"You don't need my help." Josephine felt broken down.

"I need your love and guidance. I do need you, aunt Josephine. You need me too. We are all we have left."

"You have me always, niece." She got up sounding like her normal self again. Sophia got up as well.

"Did God truly promise me this?" Josephine asked feeling hopeful.

"You know that he did and he does not lie," Sophia answered.

"Then, this is done. I will not kill you, Priest, nor will I leave you in one piece," Josephine said, then grabbed God's lightning bolt as God himself willed Sophia's sword out of her way. Josephine slashed Priest twice across his face removing his right eye leaving behind a scar in the form of an X, God's symbol. She put Priest's eye on her left palm and there it forever remained.

"Your eye is mine now and I can see all that you do. If you ever move against God again or harm another human being, I will destroy you," Josephine vowed, then she and Sophia vanished leaving Priest alone surrounded by the fire that continued to burn everything around him except for the church. Jesus' stone footprints disappeared, leaving no path to or from the church. Priest was to spend the remainder of his days alone in the church he failed.

Sophia and Josephine came to the house of Simon and Elle Norah, the ones responsible for the death of Anius. Elle and Simon were inside with their two daughters and their infant son Pascal who was now six weeks old. Sophia paced for a moment outside of their home. Josephine stayed close, silent, leaning on an oak tree.

"What troubles you?" she finally asked.

"That man in there killed him. He killed my father. I've waited for this moment, agonized over it—" she paused. "There has been so much bloodshed leading up to this. I want to end it but I don't know how or what happens next." Sophia felt herself losing control.

"You do not have to do this, not now or ever. It won't bring any of them back. I am with you either way." She kissed her cheek, then waited for Sophia to decide. Sophia went to Elle and Simon's door and walked inside. Josephine waited outside at first listening to the screams of the terrified family. She too felt the weight of all that transpired since her family's demise and longed for the blood vendetta to be over. She lingered a moment longer, then slowly crept toward the house already knowing what awaited her inside.

The walls of the small cottage were covered with Simon Norah's blood. His wife and daughters clutched each other tightly screaming and begging Sophia to stop attacking him. She had ripped his arm off and left him bleeding at her feet while she sat in his place at his dining room table eating his meal. Pascal screamed from their bedroom. Sophia allowed Elle Norah to fetch the child.

"Please don't hurt my daughters, not my girls, they are innocent. Here, take him. You can have Pascal. He's worthless. He was born blind. All he does is cry," Elle Norah pleaded, pointing her son toward Sophia when she entered the room.

"Let me get this straight. You are offering me your son who you deem unworthy because he is blind?" Sophia asked baffled.

"Yes, yes, he is the one you want," Elle Norah answered coldly. Sophia could sense that this woman really had no love for her own son. She roughly handed her baby to Sophia, glad to be rid of him. Josephine giggled when she saw the peculiar look on Sophia's face as she held Pascal. This was the first time she had ever held a baby. Pascal was smellier than she expected. He instantly stopped crying in her arms. His pupils were a milky white color. He was completely blind yet looked directly at her as if he could see her. He smiled and twisted her hair in his tiny fingers. This made Sophia feel a sense of joy that she hid from everyone else. She handed the baby to Josephine.

"There was no one kinder and more merciful as Anius was and if there is even an ounce of him in you, I believe that you will do the right thing and choose mercy," Elle Norah begged Sophia on her knees while Simon laughed. His daughters were so afraid they could not stop crying. Sophia consoled them.

"Sweet little girls, it is awfully late, kiss your mother and father goodnight, then off to bed you go. Don't forget to say your prayers," she calmly said to the girls and they quickly obeyed. Their mother was relieved when she heard her girls say their prayers, then fall silent, asleep. Josephine sat at the table with Pascal still in her arms.

"Thank you! Thank you so much for sparing them." Elle Norah hugged her.

"Do not thank me, conniver, for your children are already dead. Letting them die peacefully in their sleep was the extent of my mercy. I did that only because of the love and respect that I have for my father who you slaughtered." Sophia's tone remained eerily calm. Elle Norah released her, then ran into her daughter's room and started screaming when she saw that Sophia was telling the truth and her daughters were in fact dead. Sophia searched Simon's soul for any emotion over the death of his children but she found nothing. He had no love for his children, especially Pascal. He despised him and had wanted to take his life when he was born but was too weak to commit the act. Elle Norah returned to the room hysterically. She picked up the knife from her plate, then lunged at Sophia. She turned and looked at her. Elle Norah was instantly blinded. She dropped the knife clutching her eyes.

"Elle Norah, you will spend your eternity in hell blind just like the son you have forsaken," Sophia commanded and it was so. Never again did she have sight. Simon continued to laugh maniacally.

"There she is! You really are your father's daughter," he said smiling wickedly.

"Simon Norah, I've had a long time to think about how I would make you suffer. You! The scum that murdered my father. Nothing that I can imagine will suffice. Especially after I've seen how cruel you are to your own. Your bloodline is tainted. You all deserve to be eradicated!" she yelled in his face. Simon was very amused.

"You are the princess of suffering. Don't you know that?" He laughed. His words and behavior made Sophia feel uneasy. She attempted to read his thoughts but she could not.

"Sophia!" Josephine called out but she ignored her. She wanted to hear him out.

"Danara, poor sweet Danara. Your mother was indeed splendid, as kind and as loving as she was beautiful. Once that demon's blood got a hold of her, she was never the same. After she became a savage animal, she had to be put down. We did exactly what your father ordered us to do." Simon Norah told the truth, speaking of her birth father Lucifer.

"Stop this, Sophia! End him now!" Josephine demanded.

"*Liar!* My father would never order such a thing," she shouted confused.

"Yes, he did. Oh, you truly do not understand, empress of evil. Your father—" he began but this time, Josephine did not allow him to continue. She willed his body off of the ground, then his mouth opened wide as she ordered his tongue to extend, then wrap around his neck choking him. She was livid. She knew that he was about to expose the truth of Sophia's lineage and she was not going to allow that.

"Let him speak!" Sophia said firmly.

"*No*! He never gets to speak again!" Josephine yelled causing the cottage to shift. She had forgotten the infant Pascal was still in her arms but instinctively held on tight to him.

"You assassinated my family, beheaded your king, then laughed in his daughter's face and attempt to cause her more pain by spewing lies. No! You will choke on your words," Josephine said as Simon could hear the sound of his bones breaking. She was slowly squeezing him to death with his own tongue.

"Sophia was right about your death. Nothing will suffice," Josephine said frantically looking around for the perfect object to torture him with.

"S-Simon!" Elle Norah panicked when she no longer heard her husband's voice. She wept knowing she would never hear or see him again.

"Silence!" Josephine ordered her as she continued to search the room until she came upon a jar of mustard seeds. Josephine took a handful and chewed them. She picked up the same blade that Elle Norah meant to stab Sophia with and sliced her open from her neck to her bellybutton.

"Elle Norah, you do not deserve my mercy but you do have my pity. You mourn a man that did not even shed a tear when your children died. He did not plead for your life nor theirs. He doesn't love you just as you do not love your own son. Your weakness saddens me. Now I see how Lucifer so easily persuaded you to kill your own king and you poisoned your innocent son in the process, drinking that monster's poison to bring on your labor early so you could trap my brother. Yes, I know everything that you did. That is why you blame yourself for Pascal's blindness and you should. Lucifer deceived you, he promised you a son but his promises come with a price. Pascal is blind because of you but instead of loving and nurturing the boy you damaged, you were willing to sacrifice him to save yourself. You-are-pitiful! You are the reason why your precious daughters are gone. Fear not, they are in the presence of God now. Since it was you that led our kingdom to its doom, it will be you who delivers a message to Lucifer for me. He will know exactly what that is when he sees it," Josephine said, then regurgitated the mustard seeds she had just swallowed. The seed merged together forming one palm-sized mustard seed ignited with the heaven's flame. Sophia opened her mouth in shock. She had not seen the beautiful flame that her father once wielded in so long. She could not believe that Josephine was able to manifest it. She watched her aunt place the seed inside of Elle Norah's chest, then sealed her wound. Elle Norah wanted to speak but she could not, nor could she move. Although she could not see, she knew that the hand now wrapped around her neck strangling her was from the arm that Sophia had ripped from her husband's body earlier. *Such a cruel way to die*, she thought to herself. She accepted what she knew she deserved. She thought of only one thing while the arm that once caressed her and held her close snapped her neck. Her last thought was that if she could ask for one more thing, it would be mercy for her son Pascal. Elle and Simon Norah took their final breaths and died at the same time, then went off on their separate journeys to hell.

"Give me the boy, Josephine," Sophia insisted.

"Mercy," Josephine responded. It was then that she realized that she had killed Pascal's parents while she held him in her arms. When she handed him to Sophia, he was completely covered in his mother and father's blood.

"What of mercy?" Sophia asked.

"Mercy. That was his mother's final wish. She doesn't deserve anything from us but Pascal does. I have never asked you for anything Sophia. I've watched you take countless lives and never interfered, until now. For that, I am deeply sorry. I will never take away your choices again." Josephine was sincere.

"Why did you interfere?" Sophia asked wiping the blood of Pascal's parents off of his face. Josephine was certain that although Sophia was showing the infant kindness at this moment, she was absolutely capable of killing him at any time. She felt compelled to show him mercy. Not only because she brutally murdered his parents right in front of him but because her beloved brother's final act was saving this innocent child. For that reason, if Sophia was to claim her soul for her betrayal, her final act would also be protecting this child that she knew without a doubt had a higher purpose. She wished with all of her heart that she could tell Sophia why she killed the Norahs. It was to protect her from the truth.

"You rob me of my revenge, then ask for mercy for Pascal. You know this vendetta ends with him. He must die no matter what. I cannot honor your request," Sophia said coldly as she tightened her grip on Pascal causing him to cry.

"You deserved revenge as much as I did. They were your family too. That is not what vexes me. You killed Simon Norah because you did not want him to speak. I am not ignorant. I could not read his thoughts nor yours so this had something to do with what you are protecting me from. That much I know, but you lied to me about being able to wield heaven's flame. I cannot comprehend why you would keep that from me. You know how hard I've tried to recreate it myself just to feel its warmth and to feel close to my father again." Sophia was unaware of the teardrops that fell from her eyes as she spoke. Pascal stopped crying.

"You could have saved our family with the flame. Why didn't you, Josephine? If I cannot trust you, then there is no reason for me to allow you to live so I will deliver you to the gates of hell and you can tell my mother that I did what she wanted and destroyed all of her enemies. If heaven shows you mercy and lets you in, then tell my father that love no longer lives in my heart and that I am not sorry for murdering his sweet little sister in the most horrific way possible." She paused. She felt emotion taking over. She wanted to end both Josephine and Pascal's life. That was what her inner voice was instructing her to do.

"I know that you are struggling inside. All you feel is rage, hear me Sophia. Everything that I do is for family. There is nothing that I would not sacrifice to save ours. I honestly could not wield the flame before now," Josephine pleaded.

"You are a master manipulator with your words, equivocator. If truth is not what parts your lips next, I will crush Pascal's tiny heart and force you to watch me eat it before I bring my previous plan of murdering you to fruition," Sophia said listening to the whispers inside of her head telling her to kill Josephine. She clenched her first as she fought the urge, giving her one more chance to explain herself. Josephine felt this and began to speak.

"I swear on both of my brother's souls. Tonight was the only time I've used heaven's flame. Even now as I tell you the absolute truth, I know I shall never be able to wield it again," Josephine spoke from the heart. "Anius your father taught you the word of God. You know the story of the mustard seed and how having faith even that small can move mountains. Well, Lucifer is our mountain. Now is not the time for him to be conquered but God allowed me to use the flame to send a message—one that Lucifer will understand loud and clear when he lays eyes upon it. I need you to believe that I am with you until the end, Sophia. There is no need to doubt me. I know you hear the demon in your head as your mother did and as we all do. He is that tiny voice that whispers madness into your ear. When we are at our weakest, we answer Lucifer's call. For you and Danara, it's different. You hear his voice louder. It is entrancing but remember, it is also misleading. Do not let him win, not after all we've sacrificed for you to live free of him. Block out his voice. I know you are strong enough, too. Listen to your heart. What does your heart tell you to do right now?" Josephine spoke lovingly and truthfully. Sophia sobbed, then handed Pascal to her. Josephine held both children in her arms.

"We will take Pascal to safety, then we will join Dominick. He has the last of Lucifer's blood. We must keep a close eye on him. There you will rest. Thank you, Sophia. Your father is smiling down on you. You made the right decision." Josephine kissed her gently. Sophia looked up at her peculiarly.

"Aunt Josephine, you did it. You silenced Lucifer. I cannot hear his voice anymore," Sophia said relieved.

"Splendid! That means my message was received." Josephine smiled, then took the children to safety.

# EPILOGUE

Lucifer paced back and forth awaiting word about his latest arrival as his minions watched him nervously because they had never seen their master worried before.

"Where is she?" Lucifer asked his minion anxiously as he entered the room.

"This way, master! We kept her secluded from all the others. They are reacting to her presence," his minion answered nervously.

"Sire!" He bowed his head afraid to divulge the other details.

"Speak!" Lucifer shouted. His minion cleared his throat.

"She . . . she's not like any of the others. We think the sorceress Josephine put something inside of her," his minion said, then braced himself for his master's reaction.

Lucifer's movement ceased. He almost laughed out loud at first because he did not view Josephine nor anyone as a threat but at this moment, he felt emotions that he had not felt since he was banished from God's sight forever and cast out of heaven. Right now, he felt fear and regret. He began to run toward the double doors of his quarters; his minions chased him afraid of the unknown. Lucifer now regretted orchestrating the demise of Anius and Danara because now, he knew his actions caused the chain of events that would ultimately lead to his end. He looked back and saw that he was not only being followed by his minions but he was also being chased by the very souls he had tortured for centuries. Everyone around him could feel that something was stirring and were willing to break the demon's rules to bear witness.

When Lucifer reached his quarters, he had his minions secure the doors but they were unsuccessful. The lost souls broke through, then stopped immediately when they saw Elle Norah suspended in the air with her arms bound over her head. Her eyes were closed. They opened slowly as Lucifer approached her. He saw that she was blind and knew that it was Sophia his own flesh and blood that made it so.

"You must get it out of me!" Elle Norah pleaded. Her gaze never left him even as he maneuvered his way around the room to get to her. Lost souls were surrounding her and more continued to flood the massive room.

"What is in you, human?" Lucifer asked standing before her.

"Josephine said you would know once you see it. Please! Release me. What she put inside of me hurts more than anything you or your minions could ever do to me," Elle Norah said, then her head fell back and she let out a painful moan that silenced everything. Lucifer who normally would relish from the sound of someone in pain felt pity for her. He knew all she had suffered and that he was to blame. She had betrayed her king, lost her children, and left the earth strangled by her own husband's hand. God's once most beautiful angel stretched out his arm toward Elle Norah. He ran the long black nail of his forefinger down her chest slicing her open. His hand shook as he did this. Light shined through her fresh wound. Lucifer reached his hand inside of her but fear would not allow him to grasp what was inside.

"Retrieve it!" he ordered his minions. Several of them clawed at her body ripping it apart and tossing her remains aside at Lucifer's feet leaving only her heart still suspended in the air. He slowly took it into his hands carefully watching the bits of light reflecting through Elle Norah's heart. He ripped her heart open. They were all astonished by the bright light of heaven's flame.

"M-m-master what is that?" his minion asked afraid.

Lucifer did not dare respond not because he did not know what the small circular object ignited with his only weakness was. He did not respond out of fear. The knowledge of the object's meaning would be the end of him. This was the beginning of his demise and there was nothing he could do to stop it.

The lost souls began to whisper amongst each other. Lucifer could not hear what they were saying but he knew. His minions moved to extinguish the flame but all who came too close were destroyed.

"You will not say it, Lucifer, but we know what that is." He heard a woman from the crowd spoke.

"Who said that? Come forward!" he ordered. No one obeyed.

"Josephine has blessed us." A man shouted from the crowd getting others excited.

"She sent us a mustard seed."

"Wrapped in heaven's flame."

"God has not forgotten us!"

Lucifer heard multiple voices shouting. The mustard seed grew as they all began to remember its meaning.

"Get them out of here!" he shrieked at his minions. They quickly tried to clear the room but as the mustard seed grew from their belief, it became brighter and more visible for all to see. Lost souls flooded the room breaking down the doors and destroying the foundation around it. Lucifer was no longer separated from the souls he tortured and they were no longer afraid of him. They all desperately needed to see the mustard seed. He heard a woman's laughter stand out amongst all other voices silencing them. She crawled out from behind his throne of corpses. She was bloody and filthy. Her arms and legs were bound by heavy silver chains that dug into her flesh. She struggled to stand. Some of the lost souls scurried over to help her but she put her hand up and stopped them in their tracks showing them that she could now stand because she no longer felt broken and alone. She felt the spirit of her husband and the presence of God with her. As she walked toward the now tremendous mustard seed, everyone moved out of her way—the lost souls, the devil's minions, and all of his monstrosities that dwelled in hell.

"Danara, stop! I order you to stay away from . . ." Lucifer yelled, then could not finish his sentence.

The chains that once bound her fell to the ground. The mustard seed gravitated to Danara floating just over her head. A bright light shined from it illuminating only her face. A voice spoke from heaven's flame in words only she could understand. She looked back at Lucifer as she listened, then again at the flame shaking her head in agreement. The light that reflected on her face slowly illuminated her body restoring her completely inside and out. She was no longer bloody and filthy. She was cleansed and dressed in her pure white wedding dress; the same dress Lucifer defiled her in; the same beautiful dress that she designed with her mother Annalise and married Anius in. God chose this dress to remind Lucifer of her journey. This dress represented her pain, her love, and God's restoration. Danara was not a perfect person but she was loyal. She made mistakes and took countless lives. Still, God forgave her. Lucifer tried to break her. Sophia nearly destroyed her. She lost her mother, her love, her life. She was hopeless from the beginning being the daughter of rape created from hate. She was tested numerous times by God and Lucifer, felt hated by both, yet still decided with her free will to trust one and believe in only one, and that one was and would forever be the Almighty God. For this, he never turned his ears from her prayers nor let her leave his sight.

"The Creator has spoken." Her voice rang throughout hell. There was no dark corner her voice could not reach.

"God allowed my sister Josephine to send Lucifer and all of you a message inside of the body of Elle Norah, the woman responsible for the death of my husband who now resides in heaven at God's side. She sent the message in the form of a mustard seed. This seed is a reminder of our Lord's promise." As she spoke, more flocked into the room to hear her.

"Matthew 17 verse 20. Jesus replied, because you have such little faith. Truly I tell you, if you have faith as small as a mustard seed, you can say to this mountain, move from here to there, and it will move. Nothing will be impossible for you," Danara said, then paused.

"*Do you have faith*?" she shouted causing an immediate uproar.

"Even after all this time that you have suffered at the hands of Lucifer. *Do you still believe*?" she shouted. The crowd began to cheer as the mustard seed continued to grow and ascended to the highest heights in hell for all to witness. When it reached the top, it remained there shining a bright ray of blue looking down on all sinners as the sun did in their beautiful earth sky.

"God wants you to know that his promise of eternal life still remains if you . . ."

"Humble yourself before him."

"Repent your sins."

"Accept Jesus as your Lord and Savior and . . ."

"Be baptized in his holy water, then you will be saved," Danara concluded.

"She offers you false hope. This is a trick. The one that sent the mustard seed is a sorceress. Both of these whores are deceiving you. If you believe her for even a moment, then the suffering I have already inflicted upon you will be *nothing* compared to what I do to you next!" he roared. Lucifer could not help but to try and sway their opinions. He knew that Danara spoke the truth.

"Silence, demon!" she commanded. He could not contest.

"God spoke to me through the flames and said that all of my sins were forgiven and that I could take my place in heaven with my husband but I decided what he already knew I would because he knows me well. I decided to remain here with you because I cannot leave not one soul behind," she said as they all looked upon her with confusion and disbelief.

"I know many of you do not believe me but that is why I stand before you now and am no longer kneeling beneath the heels of Lucifer. Some of you are angry with God because you are here. You should be angry with yourselves. You cannot even blame all of your troubles on Lucifer. Yes, he deceived you but you allowed it. It's time to take responsibility for your actions and make a decision. You are either with God or against him. *Choose now*! If you believe that Jesus died on the cross for your sins and that no one cometh unto the Father except through him, let him hear you call out his name. I promise he will hear your cry in heaven and *he will answer*!" she said undeniably. More than half of the lost souls believed her and called out Jesus' name.

"*Jesus!*"

"*Jesus!*"

"*Jesus!*"

They cried out with renewed faith now greater than a mustard seed. Danara began to walk out of Lucifer's quarters. He was so angry he lunged at her when her back was turned. She stopped moving but did not turn to face him. Instead, she moved her hair from behind her neck exposing words etched in gold on the upper part of her back. The words read: Ephesians 6 verse 11-18. Lucifer knew immediately that this was a verse for protection and that it was written by the hand of God. He remained speechless. Danara walked out with all of the lost souls and his minions.

"*Jesus!*"

"*Jesus!*"

"*Jesus!*"

They cried out as all walls and barriers in hell came down. Those that believed were unshackled. Lucifer no longer had power over them.

"Jesus is dead. God is not here! You are all trapped here for all eternity!" Lucifer shrieked.

Those that believed in God and Jesus Christ fell down on their knees to humble themselves before the Lord, then confessed their sins. At that moment, they all collectively accepted Christ into their hearts. Lucifer laughed as he approached Danara.

"I will admit, my beauty, you have been much more of a pain in my ass than I originally thought you would be, and surprisingly, Josephine is the most powerful sorceress I have ever encountered. I don't even know where her power stems from and I know many things," he said calmly. "But even she cannot bring water to hell," he said confidently.

"You are absolutely right about that. Her powers are still growing yet look at what she has already done," Danara smirked.

"Believers, hear me! Lucifer has been banished to this hell for so long that he has forgotten that we believe in a God of miracles. For Moses and the Israelites, he parted the red sea. He resurrected Jesus his only begotten son from death for you, those who still believe and trust in him, the lost souls that have been tortured and burned by Lucifer's fire, for you, God has promised to *make it rain!*" she shouted with such authority it nearly took all of her breath. She stared at Lucifer with absolutely no fear. Her chest raised up and down quickly as she regained her breath. The lost souls now believers bowed their heads until it touched the burning ground, then they stretched their arms out completely surrendering themselves to God's mercy. They recited the Lord's prayer.

Lucifer had enough. He pushed through his minions to get to her but was blocked by something he could not see. That was when he felt it. The feeling was foreign to him because after being in hell for so long surrounded by fire, his skin became tough. He had no feeling but when the first drops of rain fell for the first time since hell's creation, he felt it.

Lucifer looked up as the tiny drops of heaven's rain fell down on his face reminding him of how much he missed heaven and his God. This vexed him greatly. He turned his gaze back to Danara ready to unleash all of his rage upon her but when he looked back at her, two angels stood before him with their wings spread and swords ready. It was Carmen and Anius. Their swords formed an X blocking Lucifer from harming Danara, God's treasure.

"Jesus heard us!"

"God is real!"

"Glory to God!"

God's believers cried out throughout hell as heaven's rain fell down on only those who believed and accepted Christ.

"*In the name of the Father*!" Anius shouted.

"*In the name of the Son*!" Carmen shouted.

"*In the name of the Holy Spirit . . . you are baptized*!" Danara concluded.

"God's believers rejoiced, cried, prayed, and gave God and their Lord Jesus Christ all of the glory they deserved. They pointed their hands up high as heaven's rain healed every soul it touched.

Anius controlled Lucifer's minions and the non-believers willing them to create a staircase with their bodies.

"You deserve a throne fit for a queen," Anius said, then kissed his wife passionately pouring his love and heaven's flame into her. The beautiful and powerful blue flame ignited her pupils and there it remained for all time. God blessed her with the blue flame to solidify his promise that Lucifer would *never* harm her again.

"She deserves for you to kiss her feet," Carmen demanded, then made Lucifer kneel before Danara. He tried to contain his anger after seeing Carmen's face restored. He knew Danara did this and was powerless to punish her for it.

"Thank you, but there is no need, Carmen. Lucifer knows his place now. God has removed his touch from my memory and I never wish to know it again," Danara said happily. Lucifer had no words to speak.

Anius picked up his wife and held her up high. She kissed him softly. First on his head, then on his cheeks from left to right as he carried her up the stairs that were made from the very backs of the minions that once tortured her for Lucifer. When they reached the top, he manifested a throne made of white oak and lilies. He placed her on her throne, then stood behind her. Carmen joined him. They placed their hands over Danara's head.

"For your loyalty and sacrifice, the King of kings and Lord of all lords forged this for you with heaven's flame. God favors you, Queen Danara," Carmen said, then a beautiful gold crown with royal blue diamonds appeared in their hands.

Carmen and Anius crowned her as the Queen of Lost Souls. They both took one of her hands, bowed, then kissed it. In an instant they were gone, returned to heaven where they were needed. Anius left his beloved knowing with full confidence that God would keep his word and keep her safe. Anius now had permission to visit her whenever he pleased. He understood why she chose to stay and loved her even more for it. This was the Danara he married. She always put the needs of her people before her own, these were her people now; therefore, it was her duty to teach them the gospel of Jesus Christ.

"For those of you who chose Lucifer over God, your hell begins now." Danara's voice echoed. The rain stopped and all was silent.

"You have all forgotten where you came from, so it is now my job as your queen to remind you. I know there are no bibles in hell. Fear not, the word of God is instilled in me and I remember his holy book word by word. Now let us begin." She said smiling. Lucifer and his minions shouted in agony and their ears bled from hearing the word of God come from her lips. Danara ignored their cries and looked up at the mustard seed now the size of the moon with its blue flame burning bright throughout hell. She started from the beginning.

"Genesis 1!" Danara spoke loud and clear.

"In the beginning, God created the heavens and the earth."

The End.

1 John 4:10

This is love: not that we loved God, but that he loved us and sent his Son as an atoning sacrifice for our sins.